1

Dying hurt.

Especially when it was coupled with paralyzing fear and devastating grief. Sergeant Eli Yates learned that lesson the hard way when his world dissolved into nothingness at the exact second his heart coasted to a complete stop. His last vision was of the twisted tangle of arms and legs that belonged to his team, men he'd served with and loved like brothers. They'd all died within seconds of each other when their helicopter plummeted out of the sky and crash-landed on a tree-covered mountainside somewhere on the western slopes of the Cascades.

Living hurt worse.

Eli remained trapped in darkness as his heart suddenly began to beat again. The erratic rhythm pulsed inside his head while his limbs jerked and twitched, their movements sluggish and out of control. At the same time, his lungs struggled to fill with air that reeked of blood, death, and . . . smoke.

What the hell? He couldn't make sense of anything while

1

his brain wasn't firing on all cylinders. At least it was working well enough to sense the danger lurking nearby and that he needed to get the hell out of Dodge—though it might have been pure instinct. He kicked his legs free from whatever was holding them captive and rolled to the side. His eyes finally popped open, but they slammed shut again after one look into the fixed stare of Corporal Montez. The realization that his friend was dead ripped through his heart like one more piece of shrapnel.

"Aw, damn, Miguel."

Eli turned his head and tried again, but the view wasn't any better in that direction. Was he the only one still alive out of the nine men who'd boarded the helicopter that morning? That thought hurt like hell.

"Is anyone there?"

Nothing except for a faint crackling noise. Eli slowly put the pieces of his memories back together. The shouts from the cockpit. The worried comments from his friends as the helicopter began to lurch and then spin out of control. The impact with the ground that shredded the metal box surrounding them like paper. The shouts that morphed into screams and then whimpers before finally fading away into an awful silence—the loss of his friends' voices for good between one heartbeat and the next.

The crackling grew louder. Eli lifted his head to look around, but he couldn't see through the thick fog. Blinking didn't help, but a flash of red coming from what was left of the cockpit caught his attention. His addled brain finally recognized what he was seeing. It wasn't fog after all; it was smoke, which meant the flickering light was fire. Those two things plus the smell of jet fuel added up to a single fact. If he didn't haul ass out of there, an explosion would finish the job the crash had started.

Panic gave him the strength to move but sent a stab of fresh pain ripping through his gut. He slid a hand across his stomach, only to find a jagged shard of metal sticking out of his abdomen. Now wasn't the time to figure out what to do about it, not with the smoke getting thicker by the second.

Begging his friends for forgiveness, he dragged himself across their bodies to reach the one spot of daylight he could see. He paused by each man to check for a pulse. Finding none, Eli kept crawling, pushing himself along on one hand and two knees, keeping his other hand wrapped around the piece of metal to keep it from snagging on anything as he fought his way free from the wreckage.

It took only minutes to drag himself closer to the source of the fresh air, but it felt like hours. Each movement jarred the metal sticking out of his gut. Panting through the pain, he stopped to strip off his pack in order to fit through the opening in the side of the fuselage. Afterward, he reached back inside to drag it out after him. He'd need the supplies it contained to survive long enough for help to arrive.

Outside, he coughed his lungs clear of the toxic fumes from inside the chopper. When his breathing improved enough, he resumed crawling toward a cluster of boulders some distance away and scooted in behind them to catch his breath. Leaning back against the biggest one, he prayed it would protect him once the fire finally hit the fuel tanks. As soon as the thought crossed his mind, a deep rumble rolled down across the mountainside, and a flash of fire and smoke roiled up into the sky. The shock wave hit him a second later. He screamed as the concussion from the explosion left him curled up in a ball and shaking uncontrollably.

Debris rained down from above while the world gradually righted itself. Eli pushed himself back upright and took a quick inventory of his body parts. Good, all present and accounted for. He was alive, and except for the ringing in his ears, no worse off than he'd been a few seconds before. A peek around the edge of the boulder showed that the fire stayed contained to a small area, so he wasn't at further risk for the moment.

So what next? Grateful that thinking didn't require a lot of energy, he stared around at the towering Douglas firs surrounding the small clearing and tried to formulate a plan of action. Maybe he should begin with a more thorough assessment of his injuries. Yeah, good idea. He started with his feet and worked his way upward from there. His left leg was fine, but the right leg of his pants was ripped open for the entire length of his thigh. He pushed the blood-soaked fabric aside long enough to discover that his leg was slashed down to the bone. Now that he was aware of the injury, it hurt like hell. But not nearly as much as a wound that size should. It was as if he was feeling it from a distance somehow. Maybe he was in shock or something.

He watched in confused horror as two inches of the laceration closed up tight and the pale streak of bone disappeared beneath a layer of muscle. He closed his eyes and then reopened them slowly, hoping to clear his vision. When he looked again, a large blood vessel knitted back together right in front of his eyes while the wound continued to shrink.

Telling himself he was imagining things, he closed the gap in his pants leg and continued his assessment. His back and ribs hurt. No surprise there. The bright sunlight gave him a much clearer view of the metal jutting out of his belly. The sight made him queasy. It obviously needed to come out, but he wasn't sure what would happen if he were to yank on it. Deciding that should wait a while longer, he checked both arms and hands. No apparent damage. Although he couldn't see his face, his fingers detected a slow trickle of blood seeping from a deep gash above his right ear. No wonder he'd passed out after the crash.

A voice in the back of his mind, which sounded just like his crazy grandfather, murmured over and over again that Eli hadn't just passed out. No, he'd died, same as his friends; the only difference was that he hadn't stayed that way. Yeah, right. Obviously, he'd had his bell rung but good, because he couldn't stop replaying the argument he'd had with the old man several years back when he'd driven up to Martin's mountain cabin to tell him about his decision to enlist in the army.

Grandpa Martin had been almost incoherent with rage. As he'd paced the length of the front porch, he'd alternated between telling Eli he was a damn fool for risking the truth coming out and muttering under his breath about "people like them"—people who died but didn't always stay that way. It hadn't made sense then; it still didn't. At the time, Eli had chalked it up to more of his grandfather's crazy behavior.

But now his grandfather's words kept echoing in his head as Eli leaned forward to take another look at his leg. The jagged gash had shrunk down to no more than a shallow cut. He fell back against the rock in shock. As he tried to make sense of what he had seen, things only got weirder. While he looked on in horror, the metal shard started shifting, like it was wiggling its way out of the wound all on its own. He started to tighten his grip to prevent it from moving, but then let his hand drop back down to his side. Hell, it wasn't as if he wanted to shove the damn thing back in. On the other hand, he didn't want to bleed to death, either. Who knew what kind of internal damage it had caused on its way in?

When the shard finally popped all the way out, a warm ooze of blood poured onto his skin. He gingerly lifted the hem of his shirt, expecting the worst. Using his sleeve, he wiped the blood away. Just as with his leg wound, the hole was sealing shut by itself.

"Son of a bitch, has the whole fucking world gone crazy?"

Seriously, what the hell was happening here? And what came next? With all the noise inside the chopper, he had no idea if the pilots had time to issue a Mayday call. If headquarters had been tracking their flight through whatever kind of recorder there'd been on board, was that still happening now that everything had gone up in smoke?

Come to think of it, he wasn't sure he wanted to be found. How could he explain why he alone had survived the crash? At the rate his body was healing itself, he wouldn't even have a scratch left to show the medics when they arrived. There was always a big investigation when an aircraft went down. He could just picture some idiot reporter getting wind of his freakish recovery and running with the story. And wouldn't the army brass love seeing the face of a soldier smeared all over the tabloids?

Panic made it difficult to think logically. Was he really going to wait for the authorities to arrive? The answer to that question was surprisingly easy—no, he wasn't. In fact, hell no. He couldn't stick around to see what happened. If he told the truth, that he'd died but come back from it, they'd lock him in a loony bin somewhere. He'd be shut away forever.

Yeah, he could always lie, but what story could he tell that wouldn't raise red flags? Maybe claim to have somehow been thrown clear of the helicopter before it crashed, but there was no way they'd buy that explanation, either. He would've still been hurt. Parachuting out before anything went wrong might be feasible, but what could he say when they asked to see the parachute or, better yet, how had he known that something bad was going to happen?

That left him no choice but to make a run for it. He reached for the pack he'd dragged from the wreckage. First thing, he ate a couple of protein bars, then washed them down with one of the bottles of water he'd tucked inside before leaving the base. Feeling a little better, he stripped off his shirt and pants. Before donning the clean set from the pack, he used his T-shirt and another bottle of water to scrub away as much of the dried blood and dirt as he could, especially off his face.

Time was running out, and he really needed to get moving. Before heading down the mountain, he would stop long enough to throw bits and pieces of his bloody uniform into the still-burning fire. He hoped the scraps would be enough to convince the investigators that he'd died there, too. In some ways, that was true. No way he could let himself be found, not once he left the crash site. Before leaving, he had one more thing to do. Walking back toward the helicopter, he spotted something on the ground and stopped to pick up Montez's mirrored sunglasses. He paused for several seconds before continuing to the wreckage. There, not wanting to see what the explosion had done to his friends' remains, he kept his gaze centered on the flames and tried to find some way to say good-bye to his team.

His voice came out gravelly from shock and smoke; dark fumes still billowed off the wreckage.

"Guys, how the hell did this happen? Doesn't seem fair that we all survived so many tours in the worst hellholes this planet has to offer only to have things end like this. But as you always said, Montez, shit happens."

He stared at the bent and twisted sunglasses in his hand, picturing Montez's familiar grin in his head. He'd give anything to see it one more time. "I love you all like the brothers I never has, and it's been my honor to serve with each and every one of you. Rest in peace."

The buzz of an airplane overhead reminded him that this was no time to linger. He ran for cover under the firs, pausing just inside the tree line. Aching with grief, he came to attention, saluted the funeral pyre, and then walked down the mountain without once looking back.

One month later

ELI JERKED AWAKE, pulse pounding and his skin slippery with sweat. Yet another nightmare that forced him to relive the day that his life had literally come crashing down around him. Over the past few weeks he'd learned there was no use in trying to get back to sleep. Giving up on bed altogether, he pulled on yesterday's clothes and headed for the front porch of the cabin he'd inherited from Grandpa Martin. On the way out, he snagged a broadsword off the wall. That wall shone with blades—it was where his grandfather had displayed his extensive weapon collection.

There wasn't a single gun in the bunch, but there was at least one example of every kind of bladed weapon imaginable. Some were plain and utilitarian, while others were more like works of art. Even as a kid, back before his parents died in a car accident, Eli had loved the old man's collection. Some of his favorite memories from that time were of him and his father admiring Martin's latest acquisition. Later, after he'd gone to live with his other grandparents, he'd missed those visits with Martin talking about swords and knives, which might be why he'd ended up on the fencing team in college.

His skills had gotten rusty over the years, but working out with the various blades was one of the few things that brought him any sort of peace on these restless nights.

Outside, he leaned against the porch railing and let the night air cool his fevered skin. Ever since taking refuge in the remote cabin high in the foothills of the Cascade Mountains, he'd been trying to figure out a way to get some semblance of his old life back. Instead, his thoughts continued to spin in circles, and he was no closer to a solution now than he had been the day he'd crawled out of the wreckage.

He glanced up at the stars. "Grandpa, I don't know if you're up there somewhere listening, but I wish you were here to answer some questions for me." That safety deposit box Martin had filled with cash and the papers with Eli's birth name on them had come in handy. Eli would have given anything to know how his grandpa knew Eli might need them.

It wasn't as if he'd ever known Martin all that well, especially in his later years. His grandparents on his mother's side had never gotten along with Eli's father, much less Martin. After the memorial service, they'd whisked Eli away to Spokane on the eastern edge of Washington State and changed his last name to theirs when the court had awarded them full custody.

They'd also gotten the judge to forbid any unsupervised contact between Eli and Martin until Eli came of age and could make his own decisions. Considering how crazy the old man had acted on the day of the funeral services, Eli couldn't much blame them. Martin had been agitated when he got there and then totally lost control. He had slammed Grandpa Yates against the wall while accusing him of killing Eli's father a second time by cremating his body so soon. The police had been called, and the situation had only deteriorated from there.

Looking back, Martin's rantings had sounded insane at the time. But now, after everything that had happened to Eli, maybe the old man had known what he was talking about. Regardless, having his birth certificate with his original name of Eli D. Jervain would make establishing a new identity a lot easier. God knows, he'd never be able to go back to being Eli Yates without risking the army finding out that he'd survived the helicopter crash.

That didn't mean he wanted to spend the rest of his life

parked on the side of this mountain alone and afraid to let anyone close. He'd served as part of close-knit team for too many years to want to go solo now.

"None of this is getting me anywhere," he said into the night air.

He also hated that the only person he had to talk to was himself. Frustrated, he picked up the sword again and headed for the small clearing on the back side of the cabin. The soft glow from the kitchen windows didn't do much to brighten the night, but he'd always had exceptional night vision. Holding up the sword as if saluting an opponent, he began a series of movements meant to strengthen his arms, especially his wrists. It didn't take long to get lost in the routine, buying him a few minutes of peace.

Starting off slowly, he focused on accuracy, and only gradually picked up speed. But as he raised the blade over his right shoulder, intending to swing it down hard and fast at an invisible target, a woman's scream, high pitched and full of fear, echoed down off the mountainside. It was followed by a male voice bellowing in fury. The sounds brought Eli's warrior instincts to full attention. He was running flat out by the time the woman screamed a second time.

Gripping the sword with all his strength, he charged into the darkness.

2

Safara fought her cousin with every bit of skill she could muster. Tiel had her at a distinct disadvantage on several fronts, starting with the fact that he was half a foot taller and nearly sixty pounds heavier, most of it muscle. He was also out of his head crazy with the light disease that plagued the people from their homeworld. Right now, Tiel wouldn't care if he killed her. In contrast, she wanted to shove him back to where he belonged on the other side of the shimmering barrier that separated the human world from Kalithia.

As long as Safara could keep her blade between the two of them, she might stand a chance of surviving the night. As soon as that thought crossed her mind, her opponent hooked her sword with his and sent it flying off across the clearing. That left her sidearm as her only defense. Unfortunately, Tiel grabbed her right wrist before she could draw the gun.

His pale eyes gleamed in the darkness with an unholy joy. "Are you going to beg for your life, little girl?"

"No."

Her answer didn't surprise him; they both knew pleading

her case would do no good. The man Tiel used to be would've never lifted a hand against her; the man he was now only craved her death and pain. In a surprise move, he spun her around and twisted her arm up behind her back hard enough to make her scream. Laughing, he dragged the tip of his knife across her throat just hard enough to leave a thin trail of blood in its wake.

Just when she thought he was going to finish the job, he shoved her away. "Run, little one. Maybe I'll let you escape so we can play again another night."

But he wouldn't. They both knew he couldn't risk her getting word to her father, the local chief of police, or back across the barrier to the Sworn Guardians, who enforced the law in Kalithia. Neither side wanted a rogue like Tiel running loose in their worlds. Before she took three steps, he lunged forward, carrying Safara to the ground and trapping her beneath his heavy body.

He rolled her over, and his damp breath on her face made her sick as he forced her legs apart. The proof that he was enjoying himself was rock solid and impossible to ignore. She got one hand free long enough to rake her nails down the side of his face. Now they were both bleeding, but he seemed impervious to pain. After capturing both her hands, he pinned them down above her head with one of his.

Even with the extra strength generated by the adrenaline pumping through her veins, she remained trapped beneath Tiel. When he used his free hand to squeeze her breast hard enough to bruise, she screamed again. She did so partly out of pain, but mostly out of desperation, although it was highly unlikely that anyone else was close enough to hear her cry for help.

Tiel lapped up the blood on her neck with his tongue and then smacked his lips as if she tasted delicious. "Sweetling, this is going to be so good between us. It's a shame that we will only have this one night together."

He'd succeeded in scaring her while creeping her out at the same time. "Tiel, we're cousins. We grew up together. You don't want to do this."

His accent thickened, making his English harder to understand. "Oh, but I do. You've always thought you were better than those of us stuck living in the darkness of Kalithia."

Maybe if she kept him focused on talking, the crazed fever burning in his gaze would fade away long enough for her to escape. "That's not true! I've never thought I was better than anyone. Besides, I was only a child, hardly even walking yet, when my father and grandfather brought me here to live."

Wrong thing to say. His pale face flushed with rage. "Yet they left me behind, knowing the same illness that drove your mother to die on a Paladin's sword also ran strong in my bloodline."

His fist connected with the side of her head. As he hauled his arm back to swing again, a deep voice rang out across the clearing.

"Hit her again, and you'll lose that arm for good!"

Tiel surged up to his feet to plant himself between Safara and the intruder. "This woman is mine. Find your own."

She took advantage of Tiel's inattention to scramble backward. When he realized she was heading right for her sword, he kicked it out of reach, leaving her gun as her only defense once more. She'd never had to shoot anyone and hated to start now. Regardless, she wouldn't hesitate to pull the trigger if he came after her again. It was tempting to run away while his attention was split between her and the second man, but she couldn't leave her would-be rescuer to face Tiel alone.

The man circled around the edge of the clearing to get closer to her. When she got a good look at him, her fear jumped to a whole new level. He was a Paladin, one of the human warriors who made it their life's mission to keep her people from crossing into this world from Kalithia. Had to be. Considering his incredible size and powerful build coupled with the ease with which he handled that broadsword, there could be no other explanation. How had he found her? She and the others of her kind who lived in the area had worked long and hard to prevent their age-old enemy from discovering their existence. They were all as good as dead if the murderous Paladins had tracked them down.

She had to get away. Had to warn the others now while all of his attention was on Tiel. Safara drew her gun and backed away until she reached the edge of the trees. But with her eyes still fixed on the two dangerous men and dazed from shock and fear, she lost her balance when her foot caught in a shallow hole. Her gun went flying into the bushes as she hit the ground hard enough to knock the wind out of her. Gasping for breath, she tried to stand, only to fall on her ass again when her ankle gave out on her. Damn, could this night get any worse?

Waiting for the pain to fade, and hidden behind the thick trunk of a tree, she stared across the clearing to where the two men were now locked in battle with their swords. If the fight hadn't been so deadly, it would've almost been a thing of beauty. Her cousin was lighter on his feet as he swung his curved Kalith-style blade hard and fast. The stranger's technique had less finesse and more brute strength as he blocked each of Tiel's blows with ease, gradually forcing her cousin to retreat step by step back up the mountainside. Her cousin favored his left side as if he'd taken a solid hit to his ribs. For his part, the stranger was breathing hard and dripping blood from his forearm.

Suddenly Tiel broke and ran, most likely heading back to the cave that shielded the entrance to his world. The Paladin started to follow, but then turned back in her direction. She had to get moving, but her ankle still refused to cooperate and gave out as soon as she put any weight on it. That left her to face an implacable enemy, unarmed and unable to defend herself or warn her people. That didn't mean she would go down without a fight. Using a sapling for support, she pushed herself to her feet again and tried to hobble away, but the Paladin quickly closed the distance between them.

His big hand clamped down on her shoulder. She tried to fight free of his grasp, which only sent her stumbling backward. Once again, he reached out to capture her arm, easing her fall. As soon as she was safely on the ground, he released his hold on her and retreated a step.

"Leave me alone! I'm not your enemy." She scooted back a few inches. "Can't you forget you ever saw me?"

The deep rumble of his voice when he answered destroyed what little hope she had. "All things considered, that would be a little hard to do, don't you think? Besides, we need to tell the authorities that some nutcase is up here on the mountain attacking people with a sword."

He was clearly talking about Tiel, but she gave his broadsword a pointed look. "You really want to call the police in on this? I thought you Paladins were all about secrecy. You wouldn't want the world to find out that you guys have a free pass to kill all of the innocent Kaliths you want with no repercussions even when they don't present any kind of threat to you or anyone else."

To her surprise, he leaned his sword against a rock and knelt on one knee right in front of her, his expression reflecting nothing but concern. "Are you all right? Maybe you hit your head when you fell, because right now you're not making any sense. I've never heard of anybody called a Paladin outside of a history book, much less Kaliths. Is that guy one of them?"

His concern sounded genuine, which surprised her even more than his denial of any knowledge of the Paladins. From everything she'd ever been told about them, they swung their swords first and asked questions only if there was anyone left alive to answer them.

Right now, he was still talking. "I realize you don't know me from Adam. My name is Eli, and I have no intention of hurting you."

As if knowing his name made him any more trustworthy. He tilted his head to the side as if waiting for her to introduce herself, but she ignored the unspoken invitation.

"Okay, then. Let's see what's wrong with your ankle." He moved toward her slowly as if afraid of startling her into trying to escape again. Finally, the warmth of his big hands settled around her ankle, his touch gentle as he did a quick assessment of her injury. "My guess is that it's only sprained, but you might want to get it x-rayed to make sure of that once we get you back down the mountain."

Before she could do more than squeak in protest, he suddenly swept her up in his arms. "I live just over that ridge. Once we're there, I'll wrap your ankle and then we can decide what to do next. We can't risk hanging around here in case that guy comes back again. I managed to hold him off this time, but that was pure luck. It's not like I have any experience fighting with swords for real."

So if he didn't usually fight with swords, how did he happen to have one when he came charging to her rescue? Nothing about this guy was adding up right, but she was in too much pain to think straight. For sure, it was stupid to let a total stranger carry her off to his cabin. On the other hand, she was probably in less danger going with Eli than she would be stuck out in the woods on her own, especially if Tiel did come back. To make matters worse, it had started to rain, which would only make her position even more precarious.

Resigned to her fate, whatever it might prove to be, she settled against Eli's muscular chest. Besides, once he wrapped her ankle, she'd stand a better chance of slipping away from him if necessary. The less time she spent in his company, the better. He was bound to start asking questions she couldn't afford to answer.

After taking only a couple of steps, he spun back around and leaned forward a little. "Can you grab that sword? I could come back for it later, but I'd rather not leave it out here if at all possible."

It took both of her hands to lift the heavy weapon, but the added weight didn't slow Eli down at all. He wasn't even breathing hard when they crested the ridge. She spotted the lights from his cabin in the distance and thought she recognized the place. If she was right, it had belonged to Martin Jervain, one of her grandfather's old chess partners. She'd been in it once or twice, but that had been years ago.

As far as she'd known, the cabin had been vacant since Martin's death several months ago. Just how long had Eli been living on the mountain? No one in the police department had mentioned anyone new taking up residence in the cabin. As a deputy herself, she was pretty sure she would've heard if anything had been said about it.

Safara waited until Eli carried her inside the cabin before asking any questions in case she was mistaken. But no, as soon as they crossed the threshold, she knew she was right. The place hadn't changed much at all since the last time she'd visited with her grandfather. "Isn't this Martin Jervain's cabin?"

Eli set her down on the overstuffed sofa and propped her ankle up on a pillow. Once he had her situated to his satisfaction, he carried the sword over to the kitchen counter and dried it off with a couple of paper towels. After inspecting the blade, probably checking for any damage from the fight, he returned it to its place on the wall surrounding the stone fireplace. Wow, she'd hadn't realized Martin had such a huge collection of bladed weapons.

She had about decided that Eli wasn't going to answer her last question when he finally glanced in her direction again. "Yes, this is Martin's cabin, or it was, anyway. He left it to . . . his grandson when he died six months ago."

Had she only imagined that slight hesitation in his explanation? She couldn't be sure. "How long have you been living here? I'm pretty sure I haven't seen you around town."

"Just about a month."

Eli disappeared down the hall, returning a few minutes later with a first aid kit in his hand. He'd also changed into dry clothes. "Let's get that ankle wrapped and then I'll make an ice pack to keep the swelling down. Afterward, I could drive you back to town tonight, but it would be better to wait until morning. The road isn't all that good at the best of times. With the way it's raining right now, mudslides are a distinct possibility, so I'd rather not risk it. We also can't call anyone. I never get reliable cell reception up here, and the landline is out thanks to the storm."

A quick glance at the clock on the mantel showed it was nearly midnight already. A few more hours wouldn't make any difference. "That's fine."

He sat down on the edge of the coffee table in front of her and pulled an elastic bandage out of the kit. With the greatest of care, he untied her shoe and slipped it off. When she winced, he apologized. "I know moving it hurts, but your ankle will feel better once it's wrapped. Okay?"

She bit her lip and nodded. Judging by his skill in wielding the bandage, he'd obviously had first aid training somewhere in his past. He quickly had her ankle wrapped and propped back up on the pillow. By the time he covered her ankle with a plastic bag of ice wrapped in a kitchen towel, the pain had already faded to a more manageable level.

Which reminded her that he had his own wound to take

care of. "It looked like you took a bad cut to your arm during the fight. You'd better get it cleaned up and some antiseptic on it before infection sets in."

He flinched as if her words hit a nerve. "It wasn't a bad cut. Barely a scratch, really."

When he tugged his sleeve up far enough to prove that was true, she could hardly believe what her eyes were telling her. She would've sworn she'd seen a fair amount of his blood dripping onto the ground from several feet away. Tracing the small scratch with her fingertip, she looked up into his dark green eyes. "It looked worse out there on the mountain."

He shrugged and averted his gaze as if to avoid making eye contact with her. "Guess I've always been a fast healer."

Which was another trait all Paladins shared, despite him denying any connection with her people's mortal enemies. She didn't call him on it; after all, she had her own secrets she didn't much want to talk about. Like, for instance, her reason for being out on the mountain in the middle of the night in the first place. So far, Eli hadn't asked, which was odd in itself, but she wasn't about to offer any explanations if she didn't have to.

Starting with the fact that it was her fault that Tiel had escaped Kalithia in the first place. Her grandfather had been on an extended visit with family in Kalithia. She'd made the long climb up to the cave to see if he was ready to return. People from her world varied wildly in the gifts that were handed down from one generation to the next. In her case, she'd inherited the ability to control the barrier from her grandmother's side of the family. Tonight, she'd weakened it enough to see if anyone was waiting on the other side.

As soon as she could make out the dim outline of a male figure through the fading light, she'd collapsed the barrier completely. But instead of her grandfather, it had been Tiel waiting there. He had acted normally at first, but he'd turned on her as soon as they were clear of the cave.

She had no idea where he was now or where he'd likely go to ground. How would she live with herself if he went on a rampage instead of returning to his homeworld?

As Eli closed up the first aid kit, he glanced at her. "You still haven't told me your name."

"It's Safara." Then she added her last name in the hope that he would share his.

"Safara Dennell."

He stood up. "Well, Safara, would you like something to eat or drink?"

"Nothing, thanks. I'm mostly just tired."

"Me, too. I'll help you down the hall to the bathroom. When I was getting the first aid kit, I laid out a toothbrush along with a set of my sweats for you to sleep in. While you get out of those wet clothes and, um, take care of any other business, I'll get you a pillow and a blanket. I'll also add more wood to the fire. These late spring nights can still get pretty cold."

"Sounds good."

She meant that. His clothes would be a gazillion sizes too big, but it would feel great to get out of her muddy, wet clothes. Then maybe she'd finally shake off the last of the chill she'd taken out there in the rain.

Fifteen minutes later, she opened the bathroom door to find Eli waiting to carry her back to the couch. She gave him credit for not laughing at how silly she looked in her makeshift sleepwear even if there was a hint of a grin he couldn't quite hide. After setting her back down on the sofa, he covered her with the blanket. "After breakfast, I'll drive you to the police station in town so you can report what happened. I'm sure they'll want to start looking for that nutcase who attacked you as soon as possible."

She shook her head. "A formal report won't be of much use. The rain will have washed away any evidence by now, and I'm sure that guy is long gone." Might as well tell him everything. "But I will tell my boss everything when I go into work, though, since I'm a deputy myself, and the chief of police is my father."

If anything, Eli looked even more worried. "Look, tell him whatever you feel is important, but I'd appreciate it if you downplayed my role in all of this. All I got out of the deal was a small cut, so the focus should really be on why this guy attacked you. You might not want to pursue the investigation, but I'm betting your father will feel differently about it. If you were my daughter, I wouldn't rest until the guy's ass was behind bars where it belongs."

Her father would definitely agree with Eli on that, except he'd more than likely want to toss his nephew back across the barrier into the waiting arms of the authorities in Kalithia. It would be better for everyone concerned if Tiel faced justice in his homeworld. It would endanger everyone if one of their people were to end up in a human prison. There was no telling what would happen if Tiel started shooting off his mouth as his illness grew worse, not to mention they couldn't risk his alien DNA being detected by a human doctor.

"You can trust my dad to make sure justice is done."

"Good. Shout if you need anything during the night."

He turned off the lamps in the living room but left the light on over the stove in the far corner. She waited until he'd started down the hall before bringing up one last subject. "Eli, the last I heard, Martin's only grandson was in the army. Does he know you're staying here?"

His broad shoulders went rigid as he stopped walking midstep. Without looking back at her, he drew a deep breath before answering. "Martin's grandson died five weeks ago in a helicopter crash. Since I'm the only relative he had left, the cabin is mine now."

Then he disappeared into a room and slammed the door shut behind him.

24

3

The sun had just started to peek over the mountain ridge to the east when Eli woke up. He didn't hear any noise coming from down the hall, so maybe his unexpected and unwanted guest was still asleep. He was in no hurry to face Safara again, at least not until he could figure out a better explanation about how he'd come to be living in Martin's cabin.

Damn, the woman had played that whole situation perfectly last night. Her last question had been a well-placed verbal sniper shot, flying in out of nowhere to almost knock Eli to his knees. It had taken every bit of self-control he had not to blurt out the truth. Maybe she hadn't heard about his supposed death before he answered her, but he couldn't count on it. The last thing he wanted was for the authorities to start poking their noses around in his private business.

On his few trips down below to buy supplies, he'd planned all along to claim he was a distant relative of Martin's, the last member of a family that had never been all that large to begin with. Until last night, no one had been curious enough to even bother asking his name, much less where he came from. Obviously he'd gotten a bit too complacent, but then he'd never planned on ending up with a strange woman sleeping on his couch, especially such a beautiful one.

And she was that. Even with her dark hair wet and straggling down around her shoulders and her clothes all muddy, Safara Dennell was a head turner. Something about her pale ivory skin and forthright gaze. She was built along lean lines but with long legs and all the right curves. Not that he had any business thinking that way. He couldn't risk tangling his life up with anyone else's right now, especially someone in law enforcement.

So if she asked again, he'd make it clear to her that he was Eli D. Jervain, Martin's great-nephew, and hope that she would accept his explanation at face value. At least his grandfather had had the foresight to tell his attorney to put Eli's birth name on the paperwork when he'd transferred the deed to him after Martin's death. At the time, Eli had been mad about it, figuring he'd have to go to court or something to have it redone in his legal last name of Yates.

"Eli? Are you awake?"

"Yeah, give me a minute and I'll be right there."

He'd slept in flannel pajama pants in case Safara had needed him during the night. He normally only wore boxers or nothing at all. Somehow he doubted she would've appreciated him showing up to help her to the bathroom wearing nothing but a smile.

After putting on a clean T-shirt, he made a quick stop in the bathroom before joining Safara in the living room. To his surprise, the sofa was empty, and the blanket he'd given her to use was neatly folded on the coffee table. The woman herself was in the kitchen area, standing on one foot as she started a pot of coffee.

She smiled at him over her shoulder. "I hope you don't mind me making myself at home, but I don't function well until I've had my first shot of caffeine."

"No problem." He pulled a chair out for her at the table. "But why don't you sit down before you fall down? I promise to pour you a cup of caffeine as soon as it's ready."

He supported her arm while she hobbled to the chair. "I hope bacon and eggs sounds good to you. That's about all I have in the way of breakfast food."

"Anything is fine, but I don't want to be any trouble."

She'd already been that, and his gut told him that she would continue to be if he wasn't careful. Throwing strips of bacon into Martin's old cast-iron skillet, Eli made a mental list of oddities that still bothered him about last night's events, questions he would never ask for fear she'd turn the tables on him and start asking a few more of her own.

Starting with what Safara had been doing out in the woods in the first place. If she'd been there on official business, he had to figure she would've simply said so. It seemed unlikely that she'd hiked her ass up the mountainside that late at night just for her health. So had she been there to meet up with that weird guy for some reason? If that was the case, deputy or not, it was a pretty stupid thing to do.

There was also something hinky about the way she'd reacted when he'd brought up the subject of talking to the police about what had happened. Yeah, so she was a deputy. Big deal. That didn't give her a free pass on having to make a formal report, or at least it shouldn't. From what he'd seen over the years, cops didn't react well to an attack on a fellow officer, making it more likely they would demand to know every damn detail so they could go after the guy.

Of course, who was he to point fingers at people for not wanting to tell the powers that be the truth about what happened? It wasn't like he'd stuck around to talk to all the investigators swooping in to determine what had caused the helicopter to crash. He'd followed the story in the papers and online, but it had been barely a blip on the radar. After a few mentions, the entire incident disappeared from sight almost overnight. That was good for his personal situation, but his friends hadn't deserved to be forgotten that quickly.

Back to last night. Safara also hadn't been totally freaked by two guys fighting with swords instead of guns or even regular knives. She had no way of knowing that Eli had come charging to her rescue with the only kind of weapon he had immediately at hand. That other guy, though, had fought with that curved blade with a deadly skill that spoke of lots of experience. Hell, he'd even been wearing a scabbard for it. Who did something like that?

Safara jarred him out of his reverie by tugging on his sleeve. "Hey, Eli, I think the coffee is done."

And so was the bacon. He hoped she liked it extra crispy. How long had he been lost in thought this time? That had been happening to him ever since the crash. It was like he got caught up in endless loops of questions and memories. Sometimes he lost a few seconds, sometimes far more. He grabbed a pair of mugs down off the shelf and filled them with coffee. "Do you take cream or sugar?"

"Nope, black."

Safara accepted the mug, her expression almost worshipful as she took the first sip. "I haven't tried this particular blend of coffee before, but I'll definitely be adding it to my list of favorites."

It had actually been Martin who'd bought the beans. Eli had found them when he'd moved in. God knows how long they'd been in the freezer. "How do you like your eggs?"

"Scrambled is fine."

He put four slices of bread in the toaster and then cracked half a dozen eggs into a bowl. After beating them with a fork, he dumped them into the hot skillet. The eggs were finished just as the toast popped up. He dished it all up and set a plate in front of Safara before taking his own seat.

"This is delicious. I usually make do with cold cereal in the mornings." She smiled at him from across the table. "Thanks again for everything you've done."

He managed a small nod. "Anyone would've done the same."

She didn't look convinced of that fact. "Look, I've already intruded enough on your time. I hope driving me back down the mountain this morning doesn't interfere with any plans you might've had."

"No plans, but we should get moving."

When Safara picked up her dishes, evidently planning to hobble as far as the sink with them, he shook his head. "Just leave them on the table. I'll take care of them later."

The stubborn woman ignored him and headed for the sink anyway. He just rolled his eyes and let her do it, but stayed close enough to intervene if she lost her balance. "I ran your clothes through the laundry last night. They're probably wrinkled, but at least they're clean."

When she started to speak, he cut her off. "No more thanks necessary. It's not like I had to make any special effort or anything. My clothes were wet and muddy, too, so I just threw yours in with mine."

He was verging on being rude, but he needed to put some distance between the two of them. Without giving her a chance to argue, he picked Safara up and hauled her down the hall to the bathroom. He set her back down and stepped away to give her room to maneuver. "Wait here a second and I'll get your clothes. As soon as you're dressed, we'll head for town."

But before he did that, he wanted to ask one question. He leaned his shoulder back against the wall. "I never thought to ask. Where did you leave your ATV parked?"

Safara frowned and blinked her eyes a couple of times. "What makes you think I drove an ATV?"

The corner of his mouth quirked up in a half smile. "If you'd driven a regular car, you would've had to leave it parked on the side of road someplace down below, which would've left you a hell of a hike up to where I found you. That leaves either an ATV or a dirt bike. My gut says it was an ATV."

He crossed his arms over his chest and watched her. "Am I wrong?"

"No."

The single word was said grudgingly. She clearly didn't want to say anything more on the subject, but she finally added, "It's parked in a clearing about a quarter mile south of where you found me. It's safe right where it is for now. My father will drive me back up to retrieve it when he has time."

She looked as if she were bracing herself for further interrogation, but he walked away. The less he knew about why she'd been on the mountain, the better. Besides, if he didn't press her for answers, maybe she would afford him the same courtesy.

A few seconds later, he handed Safara her clothes and disappeared into his bedroom to get dressed. The sooner he was shed of her company, the better.

SAFARA BRACED HERSELF as Eli drove down the mountain with reckless abandon. His truck was an older model equipped with four-wheel drive, which made it well suited for traveling the narrow dirt road. That didn't mean she didn't feel every rut, rock, and bump that he hit. Ordinarily, his driving wouldn't have bothered her, but her ankle still ached like crazy and all this jolting wasn't helping.

They were almost to the paved road that would take them the rest of the way into Ridgewick, the nearby town where she lived. It would be good to get home, but the same couldn't be said about reporting to headquarters. Telling her father everything that happened last night was not going to be any fun at all. At least she could count on him to hold both his tongue and his temper until the two of them were alone. No way he'd risk revealing any of their secrets in front of a total stranger. Regardless, it would be interesting to see how her father reacted to Eli.

Would he take one look at him and think *Paladin* like she had? She still had her suspicions about Eli's true nature despite his claims to have no idea what she was talking about. Maybe her father would tell her she was imagining things, but then his first glimpse of Eli wouldn't be of him charging through the forest with a broadsword in hand. The image still had the power to make her shiver even if not all of her reaction was due to fear.

No, honesty made her admit that there was also a hefty dose of feminine admiration of an alpha male in his prime in the mix. In fact, she couldn't remember the last time she'd reacted so strongly to any man. Maybe never. She was almost hyperaware of his well-defined muscles, especially the way his powerful shoulders took up way too much room in the cab of the truck. And then there were those gorgeous green eyes that held intriguing hints of dark secrets. She also liked the way his rare smiles softened the hard edges of his face and made him look far more approachable. Too bad he was off-limits for her.

What was he thinking about so hard that had him frowning like that? Eli hadn't said more than a handful of words since he'd insisted on carrying her out to his vehicle, but he'd glanced in her direction three times in as many minutes.

If he didn't spit out whatever was bothering him soon, she would have to find a way to drag it out of him. She was about to do just that when he finally spoke up. "Were you one of the cops who investigated Martin's death?"

"No, I wasn't involved. Why do you ask?"

"At the time, Martin's grandson was told the old man had been found dead from multiple lacerations somewhere in the mountains. They were investigating, and the last word was that they had no suspects or explanation for why he was out there in the first place. They did say that the local medical examiner and at least one of the cops who found him thought it might've been a bear or cougar attack, but the jury was still out on that. I was just wondering how I would go about finding out what they finally decided. It won't change anything, of course. I just wondered what actually happened."

His words set off major alarms in her head. If she was reading between the lines correctly, there was a good chance old Martin had been killed by an Other. That's what the Paladins called anyone from Kalithia who crossed over into this world out of their head with the light disease. Just as with Tiel, the illness drove its victims crazy with the need to kill anyone who crossed their path. Paladins spent their entire lives guarding the most active stretches of the barrier, either killing the Others or shoving them back into their own world.

She had to tell Eli something. "Since his body was found outside of the city limits, it would've been the county sheriff's department that responded."

Eli frowned. "So does that mean neither you nor your father would have access to their files?"

"We have a good relationship with the guys who patrol this area. They might let us have a peek at their report if you want me to ask them."

They'd reached the end of the dirt road. He remained silent as he checked for oncoming traffic before pulling out onto the two-lane highway. Once they were under way again, he glanced at her.

"Thanks for offering, but don't bother. I was just curious."

She did her best to match his casual attitude. "Let me know if you change your mind."

"I will."

Three miles later, they reached the first scattering of houses on the outskirts of Ridgewick. Eli slowed down to the posted speed limit. "The police station is in the same building as the mayor's office, isn't it? That brick building about three blocks east of the stop sign in the middle of town?"

She couldn't help but grin. Everybody she knew gave directions based on the only four-way stop in the entire town of Ridgewick. "Yep, the door is in the rear of the building, so you'll want to drive around back."

Her father was just getting out of his cruiser when they pulled into the parking lot. He frowned big-time the second he spotted her riding shotgun in Eli's truck. Rather than waiting for Safara to come to him, he crossed the parking lot to open her door for her. "Where the hell have you been? And why haven't you been answering your phone?"

"Hello to you, too, Dad. And can't we wait until we're inside before you start the inquisition?"

She slid out of the seat, moving slowly as she tried putting weight on her foot. When she winced, her dad grabbed her arm to support her. "What happened? Are you all right?"

"I'm fine except for a sprained ankle. I'll explain everything once I get inside and off my feet. A big cup of coffee and a couple of aspirin wouldn't hurt, either."

By that point, Eli had joined them on her side of the truck, but introductions could wait a little longer. Once again, she tried walking on her own. After only two halting steps, a muttered curse word and something about God saving Eli from stubborn women served as her only warning before a pair of strong arms swung her up off the ground. The shocked expression on her father's face was priceless, but at least he had the good sense to go with the flow for the moment. He trotted ahead to the door to the police station and held it opened while Eli carried her inside.

She pointed toward her desk in the corner. Eli plopped her down on the chair and then stepped back out of the way. It was testament to how well her father knew her that he had yet to ask any of the questions that had to be clogging up his brain right about now. Instead, he'd headed directly into the break room.

She waited until he was out of hearing before she whispered, "Brace yourself, big guy. I'm guessing Dad is not in the best of moods today."

The words were barely out of her mouth when the man in question came marching back with three mugs of steaming hot coffee. He set them down on her desk with a little more force than absolutely necessary and then tossed her a bottle of aspirin.

"Okay, Daughter. You're sitting down. You've got your coffee and pain meds. Now talk, starting with telling me who the hell this guy is."

She smiled up at Eli. "And so it begins."

To her surprise, he winked at her before he stuck his hand out toward her father. "Nice to meet you, Mr. Dennell. I'm the man your daughter spent the night with."

TWO HOURS LATER, Eli was still chuckling about Safara's

35

outrage over the way he'd introduced himself to her father. Chief Dennell hadn't been any happier about it than his daughter was, but eventually he'd introduced himself properly as Eli Jervain, and the discussion had gotten back on track. Not that Eli was particularly satisfied with what he'd learned.

Or actually, hadn't learned. He still didn't know why Safara had been up on the mountain in the first place. He also suspected both Dennells knew far more about her attacker than they let on. It was hard to tell if they'd closed ranks because it involved an open investigation or if they were hiding something far more sinister. Either way, he'd clearly been an outsider, one they weren't ready to trust with any secrets. He understood how they felt. After all, he hadn't exactly rushed to share his own story with them.

For now, all he could think about was getting back to the cabin and kicking back with a couple of beers. But as he rounded the last curve in the narrow road that dead-ended at the cabin, his carefully made plans blew up in his face.

An unfamiliar car was parked out front, and a man in a uniform stood on the porch facing the living room window. His hands were cupped on either side of his face as he peered through the glass, probably to block out the glare of the late afternoon sun. At the sound of the truck rolling to a stop, the man immediately turned around.

Eli finally made sense of what his eyes had been trying to tell him. This was no random visitor. He couldn't have been that lucky. No, this man was all too familiar from the way he carried himself with authority to his light brown hair cut military short. He was Eli's commanding officer. More than that, he was a friend. At least he had been in Eli's old life.

So far, there was no indication that the man had recognized Eli in return. Was it too late to head right back down the mountain? Yeah, probably. Besides, Eli was no coward. If the army had tracked him down, he wouldn't run.

He drew a deep breath and climbed out of the truck. "Hi, Major. What brings you to these parts?"

Recognition wasn't long in coming. Mike Voss's expression went from friendly to furious in a heartbeat. He stalked over to where Eli stood waiting. "You bastard, what have you done? Eight good men died on that mountainside, men who trusted you. They were my friends. I thought they were yours, too."

His words hurt like hell, and not just because they were accompanied by a hard right hook to Eli's jaw and followed by a solid punch to his stomach. Rather than fight back, Eli backed away and held his hands up in surrender. "They were my friends, too. I swear it's not what you think, Mike. I didn't betray them or you. I don't know why the helicopter crashed, but I didn't have anything to do with bringing it down."

Mike was breathing hard, his hands still tightly clenched in fists. "Then how come you're standing here while all of them are dead?"

Eli ran his fingers through his hair in frustration. How could he explain without sounding like a crazy man? The short answer was he couldn't, but he had to try. If he could convince Mike that he hadn't betrayed everything they both stood for, maybe there was some chance that Eli could get his old life back.

"Look, let's go inside and pop open a couple of cold ones.

I promise to tell you everything."

Mike planted his feet and crossed his arms over his chest. "I ought be on the phone reporting you right this minute. Give me one good reason why I shouldn't."

If the man wanted proof that he should listen to what Eli had to say, he would give it to him. He pulled out his pocketknife and quickly slashed his palm open from one side to the other. His friend stared down at Eli's hand in horror. "What the hell are you doing?"

"Just watch."

He pulled out his handkerchief and wiped away the blood that had pooled on his skin. The wound had already started closing up. He waited another few seconds and cleaned it off a second time. By that point, the bleeding had stopped, and the cut was almost completely sealed shut.

Mike took Eli's hand in his own, holding it closer to his face to get a better look. "That's the damnedest thing I've ever seen. If I hadn't watched with my own eyes, I would never have believed it."

He finally released his hold on Eli and stepped back. His steel-blue gaze bored straight into Eli's. "It might also explain a few things that have happened since that I should tell you about. But first things first. What happened that day on the mountain?"

The man would either believe Eli's explanation or he wouldn't. Regardless, it was time to toss the dice. "I died right along with everyone else, but I didn't stay dead. I don't know why, and I don't know how, but I swear it's God's own truth."

Mike slowly shook his head, but at least he didn't go

screaming down the road in terror. Finally, he mustered up a shaky smile. "I'll listen to your story, but I'm going to need that beer you mentioned, and maybe several of its brothers and sisters for good measure."

The tight band of worry that had made it hard for Eli to draw a full breath eased up a little. "It's a deal."

4

Safara stared at the door, so tantalizingly close and yet so far. Could she make it all the way to her cruiser outside in the parking lot before her father finished talking to the mayor? The distance to the car combined with a sprained ankle said the odds were against her. She was already late heading out on patrol, but it wasn't her sense of duty that was fueling her need to escape.

No, it was the inquisition that would resume as soon as her dad hung up the phone. The gods knew she'd already told him almost everything that had happened the night before, with *almost* being the operative word. From the dark looks he sent in her direction every so often, he wasn't satisfied with her answers. He clearly didn't appreciate finding out only after the fact his daughter had been in danger on multiple fronts without him there to protect her. There was also his understandable concern for the others of their kind who lived in and around Ridgewick whose lives would suffer if the truth were ever to come out about their origins. And finally, he had a lawman's innate distrust of any stranger who'd moved into his territory without anyone noticing.

The fact that she'd spent the night in that stranger's cabin was just the icing on the cake. Darn Eli for introducing himself as the man she'd spent the night with—although the look on her dad's face had been pretty funny.

As if sensing her escape plan, her father stepped out of his office to glare at her from across the room. "Yes, sir. I'll definitely get back to you on that by the end of the week."

He disconnected the call. "Want a refill on your coffee?"

"Sure."

He was back all too quickly, meaning she'd run out of time and options. After setting their cups down on her desk, he plunked down in the chair he'd pulled over to sit on earlier. "Now, let me make sure I've got all of this straight."

Resigning herself to a long lecture, she sipped the hot drink and let him talk. He launched right in, starting with her most grievous sin. "You went up to the mountain alone and without telling anyone where you were going."

Yep, she had. She was also a trained police officer, who carried both a sword and a gun. She wisely refrained from mentioning either of those facts, because they hadn't actually played out in her favor last night. She also didn't mention she needed to make another trip up there to retrieve her service revolver and the Kalith blade that had been handed down in her grandmother's family for generations.

He was still talking. "You brought down the barrier without knowing who was standing on the other side, again alone and without backup."

This time she felt obligated to protest. "Yes, just like I've done on many other occasions. Someone has to bring down

41

the barrier so Granddad can come home."

That much was true. Her father's own ability to manipulate the barrier was only a fraction as strong as hers. "He and I had agreed before he left that I would check to see if he was ready to come home last night. I'm supposed to check back again next week. We had a plan."

"A plan that wasn't worth a damn thing, Safara." Her father slammed his cup down on the desk hard enough to splash hot coffee onto his hand. "You could've been killed. We both know that we've been having more trouble with rogues slipping across. If your cousin hadn't been alone, you would've been dead before Eli Jervain got there."

Time to divert the attention to another quarter. "Did Martin ever mention anything about Eli to you?"

"Not that I can recall, but you'd be better off asking your grandfather when he gets back. He spent more time with the old man than I did. As far as I know, Martin only had the one grandson, but he hasn't been around here for years. He's in the military. The army, I think."

That jibed with what she knew. "From what Eli told me, he inherited Martin's cabin when the grandson died in a helicopter crash about five weeks ago."

She had no reason to doubt his word, but there'd been that slight hesitation before Eli had answered when she'd asked if Martin's grandson knew he was staying in the cabin. His answer hadn't felt like a lie exactly, but she bet there was more to the situation than he was willing to tell her.

"Should be easy enough to check out his story. I'll do some poking around and see what I can learn."

"Good. And while you're at it, Eli has questions about

Martin's death. I offered to get the report from the county sheriff's department. He told me to forget about it, that he was just curious what they'd found out."

She paused to sip her coffee, mainly to give herself time to think. "But even if he isn't all that interested, I am, because it sounds as if Martin was killed by someone like Tiel. If so, we need to increase security on both sides of the barrier."

Her father's eyes, pale gray like her own, took on a hard edge. "I'll request the report. I heard the deputies who responded to the scene were bewildered by the condition of the body. The coroner thought some of the wounds were odd, but Martin had been worked over by scavengers pretty good by the time he was found. As bad as that sounds, it might've been a blessing in disguise if it threw the investigators off the track. We can't afford any suspicions that there's a sword-wielding killer on the loose."

Speaking of which, it was past time to tell her father about her initial suspicions about her rescuer. "You know, Pop, Eli seemed pretty darn handy with that broadsword. I thought for sure a Paladin had finally found us."

She shuddered at the memory. They all lived with the nightmare specter of the Paladins charging through town, herding their people like cattle back across into their homeworld. She'd grown up in this one, so it was home. Then there was the almost certain fact that the darkness in Kalithia would eventually rob her of her sanity, sending her charging back across the barrier to die on the point of a Paladin sword.

But that was a problem for another day. She dragged herself back into the moment at hand. "However, I'm reasonably sure the sword wasn't Eli's. When we reached the cabin, he hung it back on the wall with the rest of Martin's collection."

The image of him fighting her cousin played out like a movie in her head. Eli had moved with such lethal control and power, a male in his prime. It would've been sexy if the whole experience hadn't been so terrifyingly dangerous.

She picked up where she'd left off. "But also, when I accused him of being a Paladin and asked him to leave me—leave us all alone, he didn't seem to know what I was talking about. All things considered, I believe him."

"We owe him the benefit of the doubt if for no other reason than he saved your life last night." Her dad sat back in his chair, looking more relaxed than he had since she and Eli had driven into the parking lot. "That doesn't mean I won't be doing some quiet checking to see what I can learn about him. I'll also warn the clan leaders about Tiel. We'll have to organize a hunt if he continues to be a problem."

There was no mistaking the grief in her father's voice. The same pain pulsed in her own heart. It was never easy to put down a rogue Kalith, but it was far worse when it involved family. Even though she and Tiel had grown up in different worlds, they had been close as children. She hated that her memories of him were now tainted by the crazed killer who'd pinned her down in the mud on that mountainside with such violent lust in his gaze.

She knew the light disease was destroying the man she'd known; that didn't make it any easier to deal with. The fact that her mother had died from the same illness only exacerbated her grief.

Her father knew the same pain firsthand. How many

friends and family members had he lost over the years? Too many to count.

He followed the same path her thoughts had traveled. "I know it's hard, honey. For now, let's get you home so you can rest that ankle. If you call in an order to the diner, we'll pick it up on the way to your place so you don't have to cook."

Her sense of duty reared its head. "But I'm supposed to be out on patrol today. If I stay home, you'll be shorthanded."

"I can cover your shift. It will do me good to get out from behind my desk for a few hours."

There was one more problem that needed to be dealt with and soon. "My ATV is still up on the mountain. I left my work phone and wallet in it."

"Your ankle should be better in the morning, so we can head up there to pick it up before work. It should be fine for that long, especially when no one knows it's there."

She grimaced. "Eli does."

Her dad shrugged. "Nothing we can do about that. Besides, he can't learn much from them even if he does go exploring."

True enough. She kept very few numbers on that phone, all related to her job. Any personal calls came in on her other phone, which she hadn't taken up on the mountain with her. "What do you think we should do about Tiel?"

"While I'm up there, I'll do a little scouting around to see if there's any sign of him. If he is the one who killed Martin, he's probably got a bolt-hole someplace close to the cave up there. As far as I know, he can't manipulate the barrier himself, but it does go up and down on its own once in a while. He'd sense that and likely cross back into Kalithia."

"Let's hope he stays there. Maybe the Sworn Guardians will have better luck in catching him."

That wouldn't change Tiel's fate, but neither she nor her father would be the ones who had to execute him. Maybe that was cowardly on her part, but she'd save her father that pain if she could.

It was time to get moving. "Give me a minute to call in our order, and then I'll be ready to go."

"I'll let dispatch know I'll be out on patrol, and then I'll bring my car around to the door so you don't have to walk so far."

"Thanks, Dad."

"That's what fathers are for." Then he grinned at her. "That and to warn you to stay away from men like Eli Jervain, at least until your old man has a chance to check him out."

She laughed as he patted her on the shoulder and headed for the door that led to the city hall half of the building. In the meantime, she phoned in their order to the diner. Then she rolled her chair over by the door to cut down on the distance she had to walk. Although she didn't have the same recuperative ability as some of her people, she still recovered from minor injuries faster than the purely human. If she babied her ankle for the rest of the day, it should be pretty much back to normal by morning.

Meanwhile, she pondered her father's warning to stay away from Eli. Most of the time he treated her like the adult she was and stayed out of her personal life. As a result, she usually took any advice her father felt motivated to offer her pretty seriously. She pictured Eli's quiet strength and gruff manner, remembered the way it had felt to be held in those strong arms, as well as his fierce determination to protect her—a total stranger—from a crazy man swinging a sword. The bottom line was that she owed him both her life and the benefit of the doubt. The fact that he was drop-dead gorgeous was beside the point.

She glanced at her father's empty office. "Sorry, Dad, but one way or another, I'm going to see Eli Jervain again, and sooner rather than later."

The sound of a car horn startled her out of her reverie. She pushed herself up to her feet and gingerly made her way outside, pausing just long enough to lock the door behind her. For now, she'd let her dad fuss over her a little and spend the afternoon catching up on her reading.

Tomorrow would be soon enough to get back to work and start solving the mystery of Eli Jervain.

"SIT DOWN, MAJOR, while I get us a couple of beers. Are you hungry? I've got sandwich makings."

"A sandwich sounds good about now. And, by the way, can the formality. I'm here as your friend, not your commanding officer." Mike sank down on the sofa with a sigh. "Damn, this feels good. I took a red-eye from D.C. and got in at oh dark thirty this morning. Before that, I was in Europe for a week. I drove straight here as soon as I landed, and I'm feeling every mile I traveled."

Eli set the beer within easy reach of his friend. "After we eat, you can catch some shut-eye. We'll talk later when you've had a chance to unscramble your brain from all the time zone changes. In fact, think about spending the night. I can thaw steaks for dinner."

His friend didn't hesitate. "I might take you up on that. The powers that be know I planned to take a couple of days of personal time, so they won't be looking for me to report yet. Maybe I'll crash here for the night and head back down to Seattle tomorrow."

Eli threw together a quick lunch for the two of them and grabbed another pair of beers. By the time he carried everything over to the coffee table, Mike had already dozed off. Grabbing a few minutes of sleep at the drop of a hat was a talent most soldiers developed. It was tempting to let the man sleep if for no other reason than to give himself time to collect his thoughts. Too late. Mike's eyes popped open as soon as Eli set the plates down.

He shifted to sit up straighter. "Sorry, didn't mean to drift off like that."

Eli sat down in Martin's old recliner and got comfortable. "No problem."

Soldiers also knew to eat whenever food was available. Yeah, they weren't in any danger of anyone interrupting them or, worse yet, incoming fire, but old habits died hard. It didn't take long for them to finish off the sandwiches and chips.

About halfway into his second beer, Mike finally spoke again. "Okay, I need to hear what happened to you, start to finish. After that, I'll tell you what I know about what's going on with the investigation."

As he spoke, he stared at Eli's hand, the one he'd sliced open outside to convince his friend that he wasn't bullshitting him about what had happened. He held it up so Mike could see the clear evidence that the wound had disappeared completely in the time they'd been together. His friend shook his head and took another long drink of beer. Eli knew just how he felt.

"We were on a training run, getting ready to ship out again. We hadn't been given specifics about when, but it was supposed to be soon."

He paused, not sure how to continue. The rest of the story would only make him sound crazy. Maybe it was time to throw in some information about his family. "It's hard to know where to start, but I'm going to back up a few years. When I was a kid, both of my parents were killed in a car wreck while we were visiting my grandparents over in Spokane. As near as I could tell, my mother's family never liked my dad, much less his father. It didn't help that Granddad showed up at the funeral acting all crazy and screaming. He shoved my other grandfather up against a wall and accused him of killing my dad a second time by having him cremated too soon."

That memory still hurt. "They used his whack-job behavior to take full custody of me and even changed my last name to theirs allegedly to protect me from any negative fallout from his craziness. To make a long story short, I didn't see much of Martin after that. I stopped by here to see him after I'd enlisted and was about to report for duty. He went on a total rant again, telling me I couldn't afford for the truth to come out. Something about dying and not staying that way. Then he stormed off into the trees without explaining what he meant."

The scene played out like a movie in his mind. "Turns out he was right."

Mike frowned big-time, clearly struggling to get his head around what Eli was telling him. "So your dad had the same ability?"

"Hell if I know. If my folks were aware of any weirdness like that, they never told me about it. Of course, I was just a kid when they died. Maybe they'd planned to explain things when I was older."

Time to move on. "Anyway, back to the crash. Everything went as planned right up until we were on the way back. There was a loud noise. No idea what it was, and there was no time to figure it out. We went from flying to plummeting in a matter of seconds. I remember screams, then moans, then silence. Weird as it sounds, I'm pretty sure I died right along with everyone else."

He half expected Mike to interrupt him. When he didn't, Eli went on, nearly choking on the grief he'd been living with since the crash. "I checked everyone for signs of life, but no one else made it. The wreckage was filling up with smoke, and I could see sparks of fire. It was only a matter of time before the whole thing would blow. I made it as far as some boulders before that happened. While I waited for my ears to quit ringing, I assessed my condition."

By this point, he wished he hadn't just eaten. His stomach roiled as he listed his injuries. "There's no describing how fucking weird it was to watch them healing up all on their own. By the time I changed clothes and started down the mountain, they were all but gone."

Mike leaned forward, resting his elbows on his knees. "And up until this point, you had no idea you had this ability? No other miraculous recoveries?"

"Not that I can remember. For sure, I don't remember ever being sick for more than a day. No broken bones, either. And I always just thought I was lucky to never get a scratch despite being deployed all those times."

"What happened next? Why did you leave?"

Wasn't that obvious?

"How could I explain how everyone else died and I didn't? Not only did I survive, I couldn't even prove that I'd been badly hurt. Even if I'd been thrown clear of the explosion, I should have had some major injuries. I was covered in blood, but not a mark on me to explain it. I figured I'd end up in a loony bin if I told the truth or in Leavenworth if they decided I'd somehow sabotaged the mission. Neither prospect held any appeal. Then there was the chance someone would want to turn me into a lab rat."

"I can't argue with that assessment." Mike stared at Eli for a long moment before continuing. "How are you managing to fly under the radar? You can't access your bank account or use your credit cards without drawing attention."

"My grandfather must have figured I'd run into problems at some point. I was deployed when he died, but he'd named me as his sole heir. I had the attorney put all the legal papers in my storage unit. That was my first stop when I came down off the mountain. I found a key to a safe deposit box, which contained a shitload of cash, a letter explaining things, and a birth certificate with my original name on it. That's why I go by Eli D. Jervain these days. It was Eli Yates who 'died' in the crash."

He needed to get up and move around. After gathering their dishes, he carried them into the kitchen. While he was there, he put on a pot of coffee, more as something to do than from any desire for a shot of caffeine. As it brewed, he thought back to earlier that morning when he'd found Safara in his kitchen impatiently waiting for her first cup of coffee of the day. It seemed longer ago than just a few hours.

"How do you take your coffee?"

"Black is fine."

He delivered Mike's drink and then stood by the front window, staring out into the quiet shadows beneath the surrounding Douglas firs. "That's pretty much my story. I've been keeping a low profile while I try to figure out where I go from here."

Glancing back at Mike, he asked, "What happened since the crash that has you worried?"

"I was in meetings on the base when the helicopter went down. I wasn't able to visit the crash site for the initial investigation, but I did get there on the third day. Investigators were swarming all over the place, still trying to figure out what brought the chopper down in the first place. For what it's worth, they determined that it was mechanical failure. No foul play of any kind."

That didn't change the tragic loss of life, but learning that it was no one's fault came as a relief. Just bad luck, that's all.

"But while I was up there, another bunch of investigators showed up, all flashing some kind of federal identification. Any kind of crash can draw investigators from different agencies, but this bunch stood out. They were dressed in identical black uniforms that had no identifying insignias. Mainly, though, it was the kind of questions they were asking."

Eli frowned. "How so?"

"They asked about all of the men who were on that flight, but they asked way more questions about you. By this point, the bodies—or what was left of them—had already been removed. There wasn't much to look at up there other than scraps of metal and the burned grass and bushes. These guys started at the wreckage and kept circling farther and farther away from the impact site, snapping photos and taking measurements."

Eli's gut was tied in a solid knot. "You're thinking that maybe I didn't make as clean a getaway as I'd hoped."

Mike joined him at the window. "Hell, I don't know what to think, but it sure seemed suspicious to me. I couldn't postpone the trip to Europe, but I figured I'd come up here when I got back to Seattle because you'd mentioned having family in this area. I don't know what I hoped to accomplish, but for sure it wasn't to find out you were still alive. That was a real surprise and damn good news."

"What do you think I should do? I'll turn myself in if you think that's the right thing."

"Don't. Not yet, anyway. Give me a chance to find out what's going on. Maybe it's nothing, and they were just another bunch of feds looking to make a name for themselves."

"But you don't really believe that, do you?"

"No, I don't, but I can't put my finger on why. There was just something off about them. Seemed like they were part of a black ops group or something. For sure, most of them had a military background, most likely in one of the elite units."

Well, damn, what was he supposed to do with that knowledge? Nothing for now. Maybe some fresh air would clear his head.

"Want to go for a walk while it's still light out?"

Mike stared out at nothing for a long time. "No, I'd better not. In fact, I'm thinking I should head back down the mountain instead. I don't know if those guys are keeping an eye on anyone known to be close to you, but I wouldn't put it past them. I'd hate to think I might've led them straight to your door."

Eli clapped his friend on the shoulder. "Don't sweat it. You had no way of knowing I was up here. If they find me, so be it. In some ways, it would be a relief. Going to ground like this goes against the grain and feels cowardly. I never expected this to last forever."

"Even so, I'd stick pretty close to home if I were you, at least until we have a better idea of what's going on. It might be nothing, but I'll let you know what I find out either way."

"I'd appreciate it, but don't jeopardize your own career to protect me. No use in both of us going down for the count."

Eli grabbed a pencil and paper to scribble down the number for Martin's landline as well the one for the burner phone he'd picked up after the crash, not that he'd even used it. After all, who could he call? It wasn't like he could talk to any of his friends. When the helicopter had gone down, he'd lost everything in his life that held any meaning—his job, his friends, even his damn name.

Biting back his bitterness, he handed Mike his contact information. "No one else has this new e-mail address. You can also reach me at either of these phone numbers or drop a note in the mail if you think that's safer. I don't go into town often, but I do stop at the post office when I'm down there."

"Thanks."

They both walked outside, the air already noticeably cooler. "You'd better head out while it's still daytime. The road is tricky after dark when you're not familiar with it."

Not to mention there was still a crazy bastard running around out there waving a sword. He followed Mike over to his car. After he got in, Eli decided he'd better say something and signaled for Mike to roll down the window. "One more thing. I had a run-in with a nutcase last night. The police down in Ridgewick are investigating, but I doubt they've managed to track him down yet. The man had to be off his meds or something, so be careful. If you see someone acting crazy, keep driving."

"Man, you do live an interesting life these days."

Mike was still laughing as he drove away.

5

Two days later, Eli swung his ax down in a smooth arc, splitting the log in two. He tossed the pieces toward the woodpile and set another log in position. He had three more to go to finish the day's allotment. After which, he needed to make a trip down to Ridgewick to restock. It was either that or resort to chewing bark off the trees. Well, that was an exaggeration, but he could use a break from his own cooking. Besides, he was feeling closed in and trapped even though he had this entire mountainside pretty much to himself. He hadn't run into the crazy guy again, which was a good thing. There was also no sign of any mysterious men on his trail, which was even better.

He hadn't heard anything from Mike, but he really hadn't expected to this soon. Funny how having his friend there with him for even such a short time had made him so painfully aware of how alone he was these days. The only other people he'd talked to for any time at all were Safara and her father. While he was in no particular hurry to have another conversation with the police chief, Eli wouldn't mind spending a little more time with the man's daughter.

Had they managed to track down her attacker? Safara might deny it, but she knew far more about the man than she would admit. She'd also been back on the mountain. The morning after he'd taken her back to town he'd gone looking for her ATV only to discover it was already gone. A second set of tire tracks led up to where she'd left it parked.

Most likely her father had driven her up to retrieve her vehicle. They'd done more than that. Two sets of footprints had disappeared into the woods, headed in the direction of the area where she'd been attacked. He'd followed them until they turned back to where the ATVs had been parked. No telling how much time they'd spent up on the ridge, but he'd just missed them judging by how fresh the tracks looked.

Maybe he'd cross paths with Safara while he was in town. The idea had him picking up speed, quickly finishing off the last of the wood. After stacking it, he headed into the house for a quick shower and to change clothes.

Half an hour later, he drove down the mountain, hoping he'd see her while he ran his few errands. If he didn't, he could always stop by the police station to find out if she was there. He assumed she lived somewhere in town. Considering how small Ridgewick was, it shouldn't be hard to track her down.

ELI CRUISED THE length of the main street through town twice, pausing at the post office in between laps. Nothing but the usual ads and bills. One more stop to buy groceries, and then he'd head back home.

Just as he parked in front of the store, a police cruiser

pulled in behind him. Good to see it was Safara behind the wheel and not her father. His mood considerably improved, Eli walked around to the driver's side of her car.

She lowered her window and smiled up at him. "I was driving by and happened to spot you pulling in. You saved me a trip up to your place."

Well, damn, he was sorry to hear that. He wouldn't have minded having her show up on his doorstep again, all spit and polish in her khaki uniform that still managed to emphasize her femininity and looked sexy as hell. "Did you need something?"

She pointed to a file folder in the front seat. "My father requested the report on Martin's death. I thought you might like to see it."

"That was nice of you." Even though he'd told her to forget about it.

When he held out his hand, she shook her head. "I haven't had a chance to make a copy for you, and Dad needs this one back. I can bring it up to your place later unless you want to follow me over to the office while I go in and run off a copy."

"I'd hate for you to go to all that trouble."

She bit her lower lip as if giving the matter more thought. "I'll tell you what. I was about to take my lunch break over at the diner. If you have time to grab a quick bite, you can read over the report there. I'm afraid there's not much in it other than the initial crime scene details and the coroner's report."

"That sounds great. I'll follow you over there."

She nodded and drove away. Eli found himself smiling as he got back into his truck. A coroner's report might not make for the best mealtime conversation, but at least he'd be having lunch with an attractive woman. Things were looking up.

SAFARA SNAGGED THE only available parking spot, but luckily another opened up in the small lot behind the diner just as Eli pulled in. She was tempted to touch up her lipstick before getting out of the car, but she didn't want to give him the impression that she thought this was anything like a date. No, this was strictly business, a professional meeting between a police officer and a member of the public.

Yeah, right.

If that were true, her hand wouldn't be trembling as she reached for the file folder. She glanced in the rearview mirror as he climbed out of his truck. Today Eli had on jeans and a white T-shirt with a dark green plaid flannel shirt worn unbuttoned over it. In this part of Washington, the combination was practically a uniform—worn by most men and even a good portion of the women.

Uniform or not, Eli Jervain would stand out in the crowd. Part of that was his size. He had to be at least six three or four, all of it well-honed muscle that even bulky flannel couldn't disguise. But his behavior stuck out, too. He always seemed hyperaware of his surroundings, constantly scanning the area as if worried an attack was imminent. Clearly Martin's late grandson hadn't been the only family member to spend time in the military.

And now Eli was staring in her direction with a slightly puzzled look on his face, probably wondering what was keeping her. How long had she been sitting there watching him in the mirror? Too long. After all, this was business as usual. He wasn't the first citizen she'd discussed a case with at the diner.

However, he was the only one who kicked her pulse into high gear.

She grabbed her cell phone and joined Eli in the parking lot. "Sorry about that. I had to let dispatch know I was going to be unavailable for the next hour unless there's a real emergency."

Not exactly a lie, except she'd actually made that call before she'd spotted Eli at the grocery store. "Let's see if there's a booth available. If not, we'll get lunch to go and eat at one of the picnic tables over at the park."

He frowned and stuck his hands into his front pockets. "I might actually prefer that. I don't always do well with crowds these days."

Interesting, but she didn't press for details. "Not a problem. We'll run less of a chance of being interrupted that way. If you'll tell me what you want, I'll place the order. You can head on over to the park and stake out a spot for us."

"You sure you don't mind?"

"Not at all. I almost never make it through a meal here without someone deciding it's the perfect time to complain about their neighbor's dog barking or that the speed limit through town is too slow. Or too high, depending on who you talk to."

Safara softened her comment with a smile. "I actually love my job, but I hate it when my fries get cold."

He laughed. "I get that. I'll eat them cold, but there's nothing better than hot fries made with just the right mix of grease and salt."

Eli studied the menu posted in the window next to the entrance. "Are their pies really homemade?"

When she nodded, he pulled out his wallet and held out three twenties. "My treat today. I'll have a double cheeseburger, fries, a chocolate shake, and whichever pie looks good to you. I like fruit pies best, but I'd be happy with coconut or banana cream, too."

Part of her wanted to say she could pay for her own lunch, but another part pointed out how long it had been since a handsome man had taken her out for a meal. Next time, she'd do the buying. As she tucked the money into her shirt pocket, she said, "Got it. A cheeseburger, fries, chocolate shake, and a piece of pie."

He grinned. "No, not a piece. I want a pie—the whole thing. And if my fries are still hot when you get to the park, I might even share some of it with you."

"Now that's some serious motivation. Maybe I'll cheat and use the siren and flashing lights to clear the way."

"You do that, Deputy."

ELI WAS WAITING by the narrow river that snaked through the park. When he spotted her, he pointed toward a vacant picnic table some distance from where several mothers sat talking as they kept a wary eye on their children playing on the climbers.

She smiled as she walked by. She knew all of them and had gone to high school with three of them. Now that they'd seen her with Eli, she'd lay even money on getting a phone call that evening to ferret out all the details. Such was life in a small town.

Eli had picked up on their curiosity. "I take it you don't often have lunch in the park."

She plunked the grease-spotted bags onto the table and set down the box holding the pie with more care. "Not with a man, I don't."

Eli looked oddly pleased by her response as they sat down on opposite sides of the table. She set out two paper plates and added two plastic forks. "The pie is peach, my personal favorite."

Eli slid the pie closer to his side of the table. "I still have to see whether or not you earned a piece."

"Fine, be that way." She peeked into the first bag and then handed it across to him. "That one's yours, the fries still hot as requested."

He popped one into his mouth, his eyes sparkling with good humor even though his expression remained serious. "Fine, you can have a piece of pie. A big one if the burger is as good as it smells."

"It is." She spread her own lunch out on the table. "Also, the shakes are made by hand, not pumped out of some machine. Ronnie, who owns the diner, packs a lot of great flavor into everything he makes, but it comes at a price. I'll have to run an extra mile, maybe two, to burn off the calories."

She bit into her cheeseburger and moaned. "It's worth it, though. I should limit how often I eat there, but I can't resist his cooking."

Eli studied his own sandwich. "I can see why. I might even stop back by after I grab what I need at the grocery store and pick up something for dinner tonight. I'm tired of my own cooking."

There was the opening she'd been waiting for. "So you don't have any other family?"

Or a girlfriend?

Not that she was going to ask that last question. It was none of her business. Really. Still, maybe he'd volunteer the information. Eli waited until he finished another bite of his sandwich before answering.

"Nope, no other family. I didn't even know Martin all that well. It had been some time since I'd even seen him. As far as I know, he never left the mountain at all if he could avoid it."

"So you had visited him at his cabin sometime in the past?"

He nodded and stuffed several fries into his mouth. Was he that hungry, or was he avoiding answering her questions? Maybe her interest didn't sound as casual as she'd hoped. Time to do some sharing of her own.

"I've lived in Ridgewick my entire life except for when I left to get my associate degree in criminology. Even then, the college was less than a hundred miles from here."

"You never wanted to do any traveling?"

She couldn't very well tell him that she'd visited another world a bunch of times. "I've always wanted to visit Europe someday or maybe the beaches in Mexico, especially when the rainy season hits. I love living here, but I do get tired of gray days."

After dipping a fry in a puddle of ketchup, she asked, "How about you? Done much traveling?"

His gaze shifted to some point off in the distance as if he was no longer seeing the Cascade Mountains that served as a backdrop for the town. "I've seen all the hot spots—Iraq, Afghanistan, and Syria."

Looking pretty grim, he sat there in silence for a full minute. Then he blinked and was back with her. "Sorry about that. Didn't mean to blank out on you."

"That's okay. I'd already figured out that you'd been in the military." She decided not to press for details about what that had entailed.

Eli pulled out a large pocketknife and flipped open the box that held the peach pie. "I don't know about you, but I'm ready for dessert."

She had to wonder how sanitary the blade was, but at least he wiped it down with a napkin. Considering some of the places he'd been, he'd probably gotten over any squeamishness he might've had about germs. Regardless, she wasn't going to complain. Ronnie's peach pie was worth the risk of consuming a few cooties.

Her eyes about popped out of her head when she saw the size of the piece he carved out of the pie. "Make mine about half that size."

His grin took years off his age. "I won't argue. That just leaves more for me."

Even with the smaller portion, she was seriously stuffed by the time they were both done eating. While Eli carried their trash over to the garbage can, she opened the file folder and quickly reviewed its contents before pushing it over to his side of the table.

It didn't take him long to go through it. "You're right.

There's not much here."

"I'm sorry the descriptions are so graphic, but I figured you'd rather read it for yourself instead of me glossing over the details."

He nodded as he went back to the beginning to read it again. "These crime scene photos were taken about a mile from the cabin. I pass that rock formation when I go running."

She studied the pictures. "That sounds about right."

"Did you know the guys who found Martin?"

"No, they were just up there on a day hike when they stumbled across the body."

Eli was still studying the report. It had to be hard to see someone he cared about described in those terms. Maybe he'd seen worse in combat, but that didn't make it any easier.

He frowned and glanced up at her. "The coroner thinks Martin had a heart attack, and the damage to his body happened afterward."

Now they were treading on dangerous ground. "That's what his notes say."

Something in her comment must have sounded off to Eli. "You don't agree?"

Great, now what could she say? That she suspected it had been her crazy cousin or some other alien out of his head with the light disease who had killed Martin? She settled for a portion of the truth. "It's probably the cop in me, but I prefer answers to be more cut and dried."

Eli started to close the folder but then stopped to study the report again. "I find it odd that he describes a few of the cuts almost as if they were made with a blade rather than animal claws."

She hoped she managed to school her expression before he looked up to see what she thought about the possibility. "I'm sure if that was the case, the coroner would have said so more clearly in his report. Besides, I'm sure he knows the difference between the marks left by knife blades as opposed to bear claws. For sure, if there'd been any hint of that, the county sheriff's department would've investigated it as an assault or even murder. Instead, they closed the file, calling it death by natural causes."

He grunted in what might've been reluctant agreement and handed the file back to her. "Thanks for sharing the findings with me. No matter how it happened, Martin deserved better than to die alone like that. I hope he went fast and didn't suffer."

"Me, too."

She checked the time. "Well, I'm back on the clock. Thanks for lunch, especially the pie."

"It was my pleasure. I haven't met many people here in town yet, and it was nice having someone to talk to other than myself."

As they made their way back to where they'd parked, she wished she knew what he was thinking. Her gut feeling was that he wasn't done wondering about Martin's death. If he chose to pursue it on his own, there was nothing she could do to stop him. On the other hand, there wasn't much left to investigate. The scene itself wouldn't tell him anything after everyone had trampled through it, Martin's body had been cremated, and there were no eyewitnesses to the actual death.

He reached past her to open the car door. She couldn't

remember the last time a man had done something like that for her. She also had to admit she'd enjoyed having someone new to talk to over a meal, someone who was both handsome and interesting. Maybe that's why she blurted out, "Call me the next time you come to town, and we'll do this again. It'll be my treat, pie and all."

"I'll do that. Thank your dad for getting the report."

"I will."

She was about to drive away when he stopped her. "I almost forgot. Did you and your dad find any trace of the guy who attacked you when the two of you were up on the mountain to pick up your ATV?"

Had he been tracking them? Damn, she should've known he would've done something like that. At least she didn't have to lie about what they found. "We didn't see anyone while we were up there. We did find the service revolver I'd lost. Other than that, things were quiet."

"That's good."

"How about you? Have you run across any sign that he's been back?"

He looked at her with a warrior's eyes. "Not yet."

Before she could warn him to leave any further hunting to her and her father, Eli walked away. A chill washed over her as if the sun had suddenly vanished behind the clouds. If Eli and her cousin crossed paths again, she knew right through to her bones the encounter would quickly turn both violent and deadly. Tiel would attack with everything he had, his illness driving him to kill anyone he saw.

In contrast, her heart insisted Eli was a born protector with a capacity for great gentleness. She'd learned that firsthand the other night when he'd worked so hard to calm her fears and then treated her injured ankle even if he'd been a bit grumpy about it. But watching him fight her cousin proved he was the kind of man who would defend his home and the people in it with his last breath. However, even if he'd vanquished his foe once, that was no guarantee he'd be the victor in a second encounter. The thought of Eli bleeding out on the mountain like Martin had done made her physically ill.

Before she could warn him to leave the hunting to the authorities, meaning her and her father, Eli was already in his truck. Not sure what to do, she drove back to the police station. Maybe it was time to talk to her father again.

6

Eli was almost to the grocery store when he abruptly changed his mind and pulled over to the curb. Fresh supplies could wait. Right now, he had too many questions with no satisfactory answers. While he was reasonably sure Safara hadn't actually lied to him about what happened to his grandfather, he was just as sure she hadn't told him the entire truth. The police report had been pretty cut and dried, and he couldn't fault the cops for reaching the conclusions they'd drawn.

But then they hadn't been the ones up on the mountain crossing swords with a maniac. While Eli couldn't prove that the two incidents were connected, his instincts said they were. Or maybe he just had blades on his brain because he spent so much time working out with his grandfather's collection. Regardless, he wouldn't rest easy until he found some answers. If he couldn't get the complete truth from the local authorities, he needed to get online and look for other cases similar to Martin's. If there was nothing to be found, then he'd accept that his grandfather died of natural causes and move on. He just wished he believed there was nothing to find.

Either way, this wasn't something he could research on his cheap cell phone, and the dial-up Internet service at the cabin would take forever if it was even working. There had to be a better option. Then he noticed a sign with an arrow pointing down the next side street. Huh, who knew a town the size of Ridgewick could afford to have a library of its own?

The place wasn't very big—no surprise there—but it did have a bank of computer desks running along the length of one wall. Even better, most were currently unoccupied. He was about to sit down at the closest one when he noticed the petite, gray-haired woman at the front desk was trying to get his attention. So much for flying under the radar. He veered off his intended course in her direction.

"Did you want something, ma'am?"

She offered him a friendly smile, and her unusually pale eyes twinkled with good humor. "I just wanted to let you know that you'll need to log in to our computer system. I can give you a temporary number if you're just passing through town."

"Actually I live close by, so it would probably be easier if I got a regular library card."

"I can help with that. If you have your identification handy, it won't take but a minute."

He pulled out his brand-new driver's license and handed it to her. It still jarred him to see his picture on it but with a different last name. Eventually he might get used to being someone else, but he hated living a lie. When she handed him both his license and a library card, she asked, "By any chance, were you related to Martin Jervain?"

"Distantly." Another easy lie. "Did you know him?"

"Yes, I did. Martin was a bit of a grouch." She flashed Eli a smile to soften the comment. "He stopped in here regularly to read the magazines and newspapers we carry online."

It almost sounded as if she really missed the old man. It was a relief when she tactfully changed the subject. "Are you familiar with our catalog or would you like me to give you a quick overview?"

He could probably figure things out for himself, but it would save time if she aimed him the right direction. "I'd appreciate a few pointers."

"I'll show you how to log in, and then we'll go from there." After hitting the high points on the programming, she asked, "Is there something in particular you wish to access?"

"I wanted to read some local newspapers if that's possible."

"It sure is. We get physical copies of a few, but you can access most of the papers that are published in the state online." With a couple of clicks of the mouse, she brought up the right menu. "This should get you whatever you need. If you want a copy of an article, just hit this button. It will print out on that machine over there."

He waited until the librarian returned to her desk before starting his search. At first he didn't have much luck until he figured out what keywords to use. After that, things got really interesting. An hour later, he walked out of the library with copies of a dozen different articles about incidents dating back as long ago as four years.

Interesting that most of the attacks happened in Western

Washington in the Cascade Mountains. There were also a few in Oregon, and even a couple in Northern California. It was too soon to tell if the locations formed a pattern by dates or locations, but he was definitely onto something. He was sure of it.

Maybe he'd learn more from studying the kind of terrain where the attacks occurred. For now, he'd do a quick run through the grocery store and head back home.

AFTER PUTTING THE groceries away, Eli dug out Martin's big atlas. Opening it to a topographical map of the western states, he stuck a sticky note on the spot where Martin had been found along with the approximate date of his death. Then he did the same with the rest of the cases he'd discovered. Once he had them all marked, he made notes about any similarities he'd found, no matter how small or odd.

There was a significant delay in finding the bodies in at least two-thirds of the cases. Considering the rough terrain where the deaths occurred, that wasn't too surprising. Another commonality was that all of them had been found in or near the mountains. Most were close to one of the volcanoes that dotted the landscape, which probably wasn't significant. After all, there were five of the snow-cone-shaped peaks in Washington State alone.

According to reports, all the bodies had severe damage caused by animals. Again, no surprise there if the victims remained undiscovered for any length of time. Most of the cases were written off to natural causes. The rest were still open, but the investigations had gone cold due to the lack of evidence. In those cases, the coroner reports had indicated the bodies had a few unexplained injuries that could've been caused by a sharp blade.

Once he'd sorted through all of the available information, Eli stared at his notes and the map. Now what?

The soft patter of raindrops on the roof caught his attention. He glanced outside and was surprised to see how late it was. There wasn't anything else he could accomplish today. Thanks to the rain, it was doubtful there was much of a trail left to follow from where Safara had been attacked, but he wouldn't know for sure unless he went looking. However, even if all the markers hadn't been washed away, it would be impossible to see them in the darkness. Come morning, though, he'd start the hunt for both answers and the enemy.

JUST AFTER SUNRISE, Eli finalized his plans for the day. He'd start his search where he'd first found Safara and see where the trail led from there. He stuck his pistol and extra ammunition into his jacket pocket along with his waterproof flashlight. He started out the door, but at the last second went back inside and dug out the scabbard for the broadsword. Once he fastened it around his waist, he slid the heavy blade into place. Stupid, maybe, but it felt right to go on the hunt armed with his enemy's weapon of choice.

The rain had stopped by the time Eli headed out, and the sun finally put in an appearance. He quickly found the spot where Safara had fallen and knelt down to study the ground. The distinctive tread of his combat boots was easy to pick out, as were the other footprints that belonged to Safara and her father. He'd already noted them the day the pair had come back up the mountain to retrieve her ATV. There was no sign of any new activity, so he moved on to where he and the whack job had crossed blades.

The ground where they'd fought remained churned up, but it was difficult to pick out many details beyond that point. The other guy had bolted in the direction of the trees off to the left, but Eli hadn't seen where he'd gone after that. He'd been too busy trying to coax Safara into trusting him to know for sure if her attacker had kept going in a straight line. Only one way to find out.

He walked slowly in the most likely direction, scanning the ground for any sign of tracks. His patience was finally rewarded just past the first cluster of trees where someone had tripped over a root jutting up from the ground and gone down hard. The footprints were easier to pick out after that, mainly because the guy who'd made them was limping and the right prints were deeper than the left.

As Eli moved over the next rise, a few broken branches clearly marked the man's route. It looked as if he'd been in a real hurry to get someplace. But where? As far as Eli knew, there wasn't a town, road, or even another cabin for miles in any direction.

It didn't help that the clouds were rolling back in. Maybe he should give up and try again tomorrow. He was about to turn back when he realized the trail led directly toward a rocky outcropping a short distance ahead. Might as well check it out since he'd come that far. It would serve as a handy landmark when he resumed his search in the morning.

He followed the curve of the rock around to the right

only to discover the tracks disappeared into a cave. Keeping a wary eye on the entrance, Eli studied the surrounding area for any sign of recent activity. He knelt to get a closer look at the ground, hoping to make better sense of what he was seeing. It appeared someone had been going in and out of the cave with some degree of frequency.

Not only that, he could pick out bits and pieces of several different sizes of prints. There was a heel print that came from a man's boot and another might've been made by an athletic shoe. The other tracks were harder to read because the soles of the shoes were completely smooth. Some kind of moccasin?

After he'd learned all he could from studying the ground, it was time to venture inside the cave itself, not that he was going to go barging in helter-skelter. He got the flashlight out of his pocket and checked his pistol one last time. Pausing at the entrance, he listened hard. Nothing but silence. If the crazy guy was living in the cave, it didn't appear he was home right now. Regardless, the bastard could be waiting just inside with his sword drawn.

Taking a deep breath, Eli ducked under the low arch of the entrance and paused just inside to sweep the flashlight from side to side. The cave was about twelve feet wide and went straight back for about twenty feet before curving off to the left. He was about to venture farther into the interior when a strange flash of light came from around the bend in the cave. He froze in position, his grip tightening on his gun as he waited to see what happened next.

A second later, the silence was broken by the sound of shuffling footsteps. He held his position until an older man stumbled into sight, his white shirt soaked through with blood. Eli shoved the flashlight into his jacket pocket as he charged across the short distance to grab the badly wounded man by the arm. There was enough light coming from the entrance behind him to maneuver in the cave, but he wasn't about to let go of his gun until he knew for sure the two of them were alone.

"Let's get you out of here."

He supported the injured man with his free hand until they'd left the cave behind. Once outside, Eli slipped the pistol back into his pocket. "How badly are you hurt?"

"Bad enough," the man grunted. He wheezed, and his face turned a worrisome shade of gray.

He tried to take another step just as his legs gave out on him. If not for Eli, he would've face-planted in the rocky mud. The time for caution was long past. He settled the man on the ground and pulled up his shirt to assess the damage. Damn, it looked bad. Eli peeled off his flannel shirt to get to his T-shirt. He used his pocketknife to cut a large square of the soft cotton fabric to use as a makeshift bandage. He secured it in place with more strips cut from his T-shirt and then checked the man for other injuries. There were a couple of shallow cuts on his arms and another deeper one on his lower leg. Those weren't life threatening, but the severity of the stomach wound combined with his age definitely were.

"Look, mister, my name is Eli Jervain, and I live a short distance from here. I could hustle home and call the authorities, but it would be faster if I drive you to the hospital myself. If you can't walk, I can carry you to my truck. It'll probably hurt like hell, though. Is that okay?"

The man's faded gray eyes were hazy with pain when they fluttered opened long enough for him to meet Eli's gaze. He whispered, "Halder Dennell. Let's do it."

"Dennell? Are you related to Safara?"

"Granddaughter," Halder said as he struggled to stand up.

Another member of Safara's family up here on the mountain? Couldn't be a coincidence, but now wasn't the time to poke at that piece of the puzzle. He lifted Halder to his feet and then half dragged and half carried him back to the cabin. Eli was breathing hard by the time he reached his truck, while his companion was either unconscious or stoic as hell, because he hadn't made a single complaint since they'd started down the mountain.

Eli tucked Halder in the front seat and fastened the seat belt for him. He was relieved to see the man was still breathing. He ran into the house long enough to ditch the broadsword and to grab an old blanket to help keep the old man warm until they reached the small community hospital down in Ridgewick.

On the way, he tried calling Safara's cell phone several times. No answer. It was frustrating, but maybe she was out on a call or something and couldn't respond. Finally, he gave up on reaching her and left her a message. "Safara, it's Eli. Your grandfather was injured up here on the mountain. I'm taking him directly to the hospital. Meet us there."

He tried to avoid the worst of the ruts on the way down the mountainside, but right now time was more important than comfort for either of them. When he reached the highway, he gunned the engine, not all that worried about the speed limit. If the cops stopped him for speeding, they could just provide escort to the hospital. Twenty minutes later, he pulled up in front of the emergency entrance of the small hospital and shut off the engine.

"Mr. Dennell, hold on for a few minutes longer. We're at the hospital now. I'm going to run inside and get help."

The old man may have nodded or maybe he'd just drawn a deep breath. He was so still now that there was no way to know for sure. Eli slammed out of the truck and hit the ground running. Inside, he caught the attention of a man wearing scrubs. "I have an injured man outside. He's bleeding pretty badly."

The man didn't waste time with questions. He ran out of sight but was back within seconds with a stretcher and two more people following hot on his heels. The three of them eased Halder out of the truck and lifted him onto the gurney. As they wheeled him back into the hospital, Eli parked his truck and returned to the waiting room. There wasn't anything more he could do for Halder himself, but the police were going to want a statement from him at some point.

Besides, he wanted to be there for Safara. He'd barely sat down in one of the plastic chairs when she came running through the door. He waved his hand to draw her attention in his direction. She charged across the short distance to where he sat.

"Where is my grandfather? Is he okay?"

"They just took him back to one of the examination rooms. He was still hanging in there when we got here. More than that I don't know."

He patted the chair next to him. "Sit down and catch your

breath. I'm sure they'll send someone out when they've had a chance to check him over."

She shook her head and started toward the ER door. "No, I need to know now."

Eli lurched up out of his chair to stop her. When she tried to dodge around him, he caught her in his arms. "I know you're worried about Halder, but let them do their job."

"He needs me."

She fought hard to get free, but he held on tight. "Please, Safara. I don't want to hurt you."

Finally, the fight went out of her. She collapsed against his chest and held on for dear life. "How bad is it? And what happened? How did you happen to find him?"

"Sit down while I get each of us a cup of coffee from the vending machine, and I'll tell you everything I know."

Safara let him settle her into a nearby chair. She leaned forward, her elbows on her knees and her face buried in her hands. He hurt for her, but there wasn't anything either of them could do for her grandfather right now but sit and wait.

He got two cups of black coffee. It might taste terrible, but they both needed the hit of caffeine and heat right now. "Can I call anyone to come sit with you?"

She accepted the cup but made no effort to drink it. "Dad was out of town at a meeting. I called him after I got your message. He's already started back, but he's picking my aunt up on the way. She lives down closer to Puget Sound near Bellingham, so they should be here in a couple of hours."

She looked at him with eyes bruised with pain. "I'll be all right by myself if you need to leave."

He wasn't going anywhere and said so. Before he could

launch into the details about how he came to be the one to bring her grandfather down off the mountain, a woman wearing a bloodstained gown over her scrubs came into the room.

"I'm Dr. Kraus. Are you the man who brought in Mr. Dennell?"

Eli stood and offered his hand to Safara and tugged her back up to her feet. "I am, and this is his granddaughter, Safara Dennell."

"That answers my next question, which would've been if you knew if he had any family in the area." She smiled at Safara. "Sorry, I just started working here this past week, so I'm new in town. I wish we were meeting under better circumstances, but let's talk about your grandfather."

"How is he?"

The doctor studied the chart in her hand. "He has multiple lacerations—on his arms, leg, and a really deep one across his abdomen. We'll be taking him to surgery to repair the damage. Right now we're giving him fluids while we wait on his lab work."

When she looked up again, her smile looked a bit tight. "He's holding his own for now, especially considering his age."

"Can I see him?"

"Probably not until after he's out of recovery. Right now, he's being prepped for surgery. I'm sure someone will be out soon with the usual paperwork for you to fill out."

She gave Safara's uniform a pointed look. "I was also going to say that we need to report this to police, but it appears they're already here."

"I'm a deputy here in Ridgewick, and my father is the chief of police." Safara stood taller. "However, from what Mr. Jervain here has told me, the injuries occurred in the county sheriff's jurisdiction. I'll give them a call."

"All right, then. We'll keep you posted as much as we can."

"We'll be right here, Doctor." Eli threaded his fingers through Safara's and gave her hand a soft squeeze, hoping the small skin-to-skin contact would be of some comfort. "Unless there's a cafeteria close by. I could use a sandwich about now, and I'm guessing Safara could, too."

"It's to the left down that hall. I'll let the nurses know that's where you'll be."

When she disappeared back through the double doors to the ER just as abruptly as she'd appeared, Eli said, "Let's get something to eat, Safara."

She shook her head. "You go. I need to be here."

"Nope, I'm not leaving you alone. Besides, you're going to need all your strength to help your grandfather. While we eat, I'll tell you what happened."

Not that she was going to like what he had to say. He tugged her along in his wake into the small cafeteria. She sat down at a table and made several phone calls while he grabbed sandwiches and drinks. Eating would give Safara something else to concentrate on until someone from the sheriff's office arrived to take his report.

When he put the tray down in front of her, Safara picked up one of the sandwiches and began to unwrap it. But instead of eating it, she set it back down. "So, what happened to my grandfather? What kind of accident was he involved in?"

It was time to play hardball before the sheriff's deputy

arrived. By then it would be too late to come up with an alternative but plausible story that fit the facts. "We both know he wasn't in an accident, Safara. I found him in a cave up on the ridge where you were attacked. Someone had carved him up pretty good, and I'm guessing it was the same bastard I fought with."

He let his anger come to a rolling boil. "So do you want to tell me what's really going on around here, or do I tell the county sheriff that you and your father are covering for a serial killer who's been active in the state for the past four years?"

7

Safara bit back the urge to curse long and loud. For the moment they had the room to themselves, but that could change at any time. The most she could do was glare at Eli for several seconds before speaking.

Finally, she forced her hands to unclench and laid them flat on the table as she leaned in to meet Eli's gaze head-on. "I am a sworn officer of the law. I have not and will not ever protect a felon from facing justice. You don't know my father very well, but he's the most honorable man I've ever met."

"If you say so."

"I do."

When he didn't immediately respond, she sat back in her chair and reached for her sandwich. Maybe if she pretended the matter was settled, they could concentrate on their meal.

No such luck.

"I take it that when the deputy from the sheriff's department gets here, you would prefer that I not mention what happened to you when I give my statement about your grandfather. You know, how he stumbled out of a cave all sliced, diced, and dripping blood only a short distance from where you were attacked with a sword just the other night."

She winced at the graphic description of her grandfather's injuries. "We don't know the two incidents are connected."

Eli, the big jerk, actually snickered and rolled his eyes. "Well, it's either that or we have multiple crazies running loose up there all armed with swords. And if the deputy searches the department database for any similar cases, what do you think he'll find? Think Martin's death might pop up, too?"

Darn, darn, double darn.

What could she say to that? She really wished her father were there to field these questions. He might not have any better answers, but it wouldn't bother him to lie to Eli. In contrast, it made her sick. She not only owed him for saving both her and her grandfather, she liked him far too much to want to deceive him like this.

Finally, she slumped back in her chair and sighed. "I know I don't have the right to ask this of you, but please don't mention the attack on me and don't bring up Martin's name unless the deputy does."

Eli picked up his sandwich and took a big bite. This wasn't the first occasion where he'd used food to buy himself time before answering one of her questions. She hoped he didn't make a habit of it, but she had no reason to complain. It wasn't as if she was rushing to tell him the truth, either. He finally washed the bite down with a swig of his drink.

"Fine. I'll tell them I was out hiking on the mountain when I crossed paths with your grandfather. He could barely breathe and lost consciousness right after he told me his name. I performed rudimentary first aid and then carried him to where my truck was parked. It was faster to bring him to the hospital myself than to call for help."

He paused to take another bite. Gosh, she was really starting to hate that sandwich. After another drink, he continued with his new narrative. "I recognized his last name and figured in a town this size that you and he had to be related. I called you on the way here, which is why you arrived right after we did. Halder was unconscious when we got here, and the doctor said they would need to take him straight to surgery. Since he wasn't able to talk, we don't know anything about what happened before I found him, and I didn't see anyone else up on the mountain. End of story. Short, sweet, and even mostly true."

"Thank you, Eli."

He shrugged and went back to eating. His reaction had her cop senses tingling. The man was definitely up to something, most likely something she wouldn't like. Before she could call him on it, a young woman poked her head into the room and looked around. As soon as she spotted them, she pasted on a bright smile and headed straight for them. She was pushing a mobile stand that held a computer screen and keyboard.

"Hi, I'm Angelica from Admissions. Are you Mr. Dennell's granddaughter?"

"I am."

"Great! I have a few questions for you."

While the two of them dealt with all the requisite paperwork, the deputy from the sheriff's office arrived. The knot in Safara's chest eased up when she spotted Will Dayson.

Not only was he a familiar face, he was married to one of her distant cousins.

He grabbed a cup of coffee and waited patiently while Safara and Angelica finished up the last few questions. As the younger woman wheeled her cart back out the door, Will joined her and Eli at the table. He glanced at Eli before turning his attention to her. "Sorry to hear about your grandfather, Safara. What the hell happened?"

She performed the necessary introductions first. "Deputy Will Dayson, this is Eli Jervain. He's the one who found Granddad and brought him to the hospital. He moved into Martin Jervain's cabin up on the mountain about a month ago."

"Glad you stuck around, Mr. Jervain. I'll need to get your statement." Will opened his laptop and set it on the table. While it booted up, he said, "I met old Martin a time or two. I take it you two were related?"

Eli nodded. "We were, although it'd been years since I'd seen him. That coffee smells good. I'm going to get a cup. Safara, can I get you anything while I'm up?"

"No, I'm fine."

While Eli's back was turned to them, Will mouthed, "How much does he know?"

She responded in kind. "Nothing for sure, but he's seen enough to have questions."

Eli was already on his way back, cutting off any chance for more communication. Regardless, Will would tread carefully with Eli. He would do his job, but he'd do it without putting her people at any unnecessary risk.

As soon as Eli rejoined them, Will launched in with the

usual questions like name, address, and phone number. He took Eli's statement starting from the moment he'd left his cabin for a hike right up through his arrival at the hospital with Halder Dennell. Eli kept his promise to stick to the basic facts without bringing up the earlier attack on her or anything about Martin's death.

Will began packing up. "Nasty business, but we won't know exactly what happened up there until your grandfather is able to talk to us. Safara, call me when he can answer a few questions, and I'll get here as soon as I'm available."

"Thanks, Will. I appreciate it."

He pushed his business card across the table to Eli. "I'll also need to examine the place where the attack happened. It would be dark by the time I could get a team up there, and I'd rather see everything in the daylight. Would you be available first thing tomorrow morning to show us where you found him? Say around nine?"

"Sure thing. You've got my number. Call if you need to change times or anything."

"Will do." He stood to leave. "Safara, tell your dad I'll let him know what we find."

"Thanks again, Will."

When he left, Eli asked, "Do you want to wait here for news or would you rather sit out in the lobby?"

She picked up their tray. "The lobby would be better. Dad should be getting here soon, and he'll wonder where I am."

They headed back down the hall. "You don't have to hang around, Eli. You've already done enough for us today."

"You shouldn't be alone while you wait, Safara. I'll stay until your father gets here."

She would've argued, but the truth was she appreciated the company. Her grandfather was in good shape for a man in his eighties, but she was still worried sick about him. If he'd inherited the Kalith ability to heal, he'd never said so. Based on Eli's statement and what little the doctor had told her, he'd been in pretty bad shape by the time he'd arrived at the hospital.

Eli wrapped his arm around her shoulders, once again lending her his strength. "I don't claim to know your grandfather, but he's obviously tough and a fighter."

Her eyes burned with the sting of tears. "You're right. He is."

Eli released his hold on her as they sat down in adjoining chairs. She missed the immediate connection, but they were sitting close enough that she could still feel the warmth of his big body next to hers.

When Eli started flipping through the pages of a tattered magazine, she leaned her head back against the wall and let her eyes drift shut. There was no telling how long she dozed before Eli nudged her.

"Your dad and some woman just came in."

Great. At some point she'd slumped sideways and had been sleeping peacefully against Eli's shoulder. She jerked upright, but it was too late. Her father had already noticed and didn't look too happy about it. Too bad. Her aunt raised an eyebrow, but now wasn't the time to indulge the woman's curiosity.

Her father ignored Eli, but there was a definite note of anger in his voice when he asked, "What's the status on your grandfather?"

"The ER doctor said they would be taking him to surgery to repair multiple lacerations."

Eli joined the conversation. "The one on his abdomen was the worst, but he also had cuts on his leg and both arms."

Her father turned on him. "And how did you just happen to be there when my father was injured? Seems mighty curious that you've shown up twice when someone in my family has been attacked."

Her feelings were already raw from worry, and Safara's temper flashed hot. "Dad! Stop it right now. Eli protected me at great risk to himself, and if not for him, Granddad would've died up there on the mountain."

He rounded on her next. "Don't you think it's a little convenient that he came running with a sword in his hand the other night? What kind of person does that? And you only have his word for the fact that he wasn't the one who cut your grandfather to pieces. We both know he's got an entire arsenal of bladed weapons at his disposal."

She half expected Eli to go on the attack, but he didn't. That didn't mean there wasn't a lot of cold steel in his voice when he spoke. "Mr. Dennell, you're right. You have no reason to trust me, because you don't know me at all. That's the only reason that you're not picking yourself up off the floor right now."

His gaze flickered in her direction as he stood up. "Well, that and the fact that you're Safara's father. You've got a lot of unanswered questions, people you care deeply about are in danger, and I'm a stranger to you."

He took a single step toward her father, towering over him by half a foot and outweighing him by a lot of pure muscle.

"You can believe what I'm about to say or not. Frankly, I don't give a damn which way you go on that, but listen carefully: I wouldn't do anything to put your daughter at risk."

Then he stepped away and sat back down, crossing his arms over his chest, making it clear he wasn't going anywhere. Safara remained frozen in position, caught between the need to comfort her father and make it clear that she trusted Eli, at least with her own life. She still couldn't risk telling him the truth about the others of her kind.

Thankfully her aunt made an effort to defuse the situation. "Jakes, let's not lose sight of why we're here. You're upset and worried about your father. We all are."

Then she held her arms out to Safara, who stepped right into her hug. "Thanks for coming, Aunt Bitti."

Her aunt gave her another tight squeeze before stepping back. Then she held her hand out to Eli. "I'm Bitti Greve. Safara's mother was my younger sister. Normally, my brother-in-law has better manners, but he's understandably upset right now."

Although her father wouldn't appreciate his sister-in-law making excuses for his behavior, Safara was relieved that Eli accepted the peace offering. The four of them settled into an uneasy silence, the time dragging past at a snail's pace. It was another hour before a doctor finally stepped into the waiting room.

"I'm Dr. Quinton. Are you all here for Mr. Dennell?"

"I'm his son." Her father stood up. "And this is my daughter and my sister-in-law."

Safara wanted to smack him for ignoring Eli, but now wasn't the time. "How is he?"

"The surgery went well, and he's holding his own. In fact, Mr. Dennell is out of recovery and on his way to his room. We've given him a heavy dose of antibiotics to prevent infection and fluids to replace the blood loss. He's also getting pain medication. Combine that with the anesthesia, he'll be pretty groggy for a while, so don't let that surprise you. The bottom line is that Mr. Dennell was a very lucky man. If he hadn't gotten here when he did, the situation would've been a whole lot worse. As it is, he should make a full recovery."

Her father finally glanced at Eli and nodded. It wasn't much of a display of gratitude, but evidently it was enough, since both men relaxed.

"When can we see him?"

"As soon as he's in his room." He gestured toward the elevator in the corner. "The surgical ward is on the second floor. When you come out of the elevator, the nurse's station is about halfway down the hall. They'll be able to tell you which room is his."

He rubbed the back of his neck, looking tired. "I'm going off shift. If you have any questions, you can either ask the nurses or the resident on call. They'll keep me apprised of any changes in Mr. Dennell's condition, but I really don't expect there to be any problems."

"Thank you, Doctor."

When he left, the four of them headed up to the second floor. She considered once again telling Eli he could go home, but she already knew he'd refuse. Her father clearly didn't want him there, but Aunt Bitti interceded.

"Safara, your grandfather will likely sleep the rest of the day and into the night. There's no need for all of us to be here, and you've already had a long day. After you get a chance to see for yourself that Halder is all right, you should go home and get some rest. I'll stay with your father."

Bitti was right. It had been a long day. Every bone in her body ached. "All right, if you're sure."

The nurses pointed them down the hall to where they were just wheeling her grandfather into his room. The four of them waited outside until they got Halder settled in and the nurse took his vitals. When she was done, she said, "You can come in, but keep it to two at a time for now."

Her father motioned for Safara to go first so she could leave. "I'll text you later to let you know how he's doing."

Eli followed her into the room, a silent presence standing behind her. Her grandfather looked so small lying there in that bed. His injuries had stripped him of all his usual vitality. She stared at his too-still figure with tears streaming down her face.

When she swiped at her cheeks, Eli muttered a soft curse and pulled her into his arms. She slowly relaxed into his embrace and soaked in his calm strength. "Gods above, we almost lost him today."

"But you didn't." Eli's voice was a soft rumble against her cheek. "And don't forget the doctor said he should be fine."

"I know, but if you hadn't been there . . ."

He crooked a finger and used it to lift her gaze up to meet his. "But I was. Now, let's let your father and aunt come in and take over. The two of us will grab dinner somewhere, and then you can go home and crash for the night."

It was so tempting to spend more time with this man even if each minute they were together made it that much harder to protect her secrets.

"Come on, Safara, don't make me eat alone. I'll even let you pick the restaurant."

Okay, that made her laugh. "Well, unless you want to drive an hour to another town, you have the choice of eating at the diner or, let's see, the diner."

She expected him to be disappointed, but instead he looked thrilled with their only option. "Do you think there will still be pie this late in the day?"

Feeling better than she had in hours, she said, "There's only one way to find out. I need to talk privately with my father for a minute. It shouldn't take long, and then I'll be ready to go."

He gave her a long look as if he knew full well he would be the topic of conversation. His disappointment that she still didn't trust him showed in in the angry set of his jaw. "Fine, I'll wait down the hall by the elevator."

She wondered if she was making a mistake in shutting him out. Her heart said she was. At the same time, her head argued her people had closed ranks against outsiders for a reason. Before she could declare either side of the debate a clear winner, her father walked into the room.

"Care to tell me what's going on between the two of you? Because I'm telling you right now, I've done some checking on him, and things aren't adding up right."

When she didn't say anything, he went on talking. "He was telling the truth about Martin's grandson being involved in a military helicopter crash a few weeks ago. I find it odd that both the grandson and this guy have the same first name. One allegedly dies in the crash at roughly the same time the other one appears up here living in Martin's cabin."

Did they really have to do this now? Evidently so, judging by the stubborn look on her father's face. "Just what are you saying, Dad?"

He ran his fingers through his salt-and-pepper hair in frustration and let out a weary sigh. "Hell, I don't know. I just want you to be careful until we know more about him. That man's got secrets of his own. Maybe they're no danger to us, but we don't know that."

She wanted to deny the truth of what he was saying, but she also knew there was more to Eli Jervain than the man was willing to share. Not for the first time, she recalled the image of him charging to her rescue as if he'd been born to carry that sword in his hand. Everything about him fit the description of the Paladins, the sworn enemies of the Kalith people. Could he be working undercover on their behalf to infiltrate her people?

Rather than say anything about what she was thinking, she changed the subject and summarized Will's discussion with her and Eli. "Will is meeting Eli on the mountain tomorrow to look around. I doubt they'll find anything useful, but you never know. Regardless, we have to go after Tiel, and soon."

Her father accepted the change in subjects. "We do, but not yet. We'll let the sheriff's department do their thing, and then we'll start the hunt. Now get out of here and get some rest. We'll regroup in the morning and go from there."

She still wasn't happy with him, but she gave her dad a quick hug and did the same with her aunt out in the hall. "Call me if you need me for anything."

Bitti made shooing motions. "You've done enough. Go be

with your young man and forget about all of this for a little while."

Safara glanced past her aunt toward the man standing down at the far end of the hall. Eli was leaning against the wall near the elevator looking as if he would wait for her all night if that's what it took. "He's not my young man. He's a . . . a friend."

That assessment felt like a lie even to her. Aunt Bitti clearly felt the same way because of the way she laughed. "Honey, I might not be as young as I used to be, but I can remember when a man looked at me with that particular kind of hunger in his eyes. You might be only friends for now, but I'm thinking he might be wanting a lot more than that."

"The more time I spend with him makes it more likely he'll find out about us, about our world. I can't hide what I am forever. What if it's too much for him?"

Bitti put her hands on Safara's shoulders, her pale gray eyes filled with sympathy. "From what I understand, he's already brushed up against our truth twice already. I sure don't see him running in the other direction."

Could she be right?

"But Dad said—"

Bitti cut her off. "He's just reacting like any other father does when he sees a man he doesn't know sniffing around his daughter. Trust me, if Eli turns out to be the right man for you, your dad will eventually come around. He also knows that if it hadn't been for Eli, we would've lost Halder today. That will count for a lot with him when he's had time to think things through."

Her aunt brushed a lock of Safara's hair back from her

face. "What's more important is that you can't live your whole life not taking chances, not trusting anyone outside of our little circle. If it doesn't work out between the two of you, so be it. But do you really want to give up on the possibility that he might make you happy without ever giving the two of you a chance?"

Safara glanced Eli's direction and could feel the weight of his green-eyed gaze from all the way down the hall and drew comfort from it. Which, on reflection, gave her the answer to her aunt's question.

She gave Bitti one last hug and drew a deep breath before starting toward Eli. Painfully aware of how rumpled she must look, she wished she could stop by her house long enough to change out of her uniform. There wasn't time for that. Besides, he looked a bit worse for the wear himself, a reminder that neither of them had had an easy day.

A few laughs and maybe some of Ronnie's pie would do them both some good. After that, well, they would see where the rest of the evening took them. Just that quickly, a renewed surge of energy danced through her veins, and her feet picked up the pace to close the distance between them.

8

When Safara started down the hall, Eli slowly straightened up and waited for her to reach him. What was she thinking about so hard? Nothing pleasant, if he had to guess. He hadn't been able to make out what Jakes said to her right after Eli walked out of Halder's room, but there'd been no mistaking the man's tone for anything other than anger mixed with a heavy dose of suspicion. By the time Safara had started talking, Eli had been too far down the hall for him to get a solid read on her response.

Was she trying to come up with an excuse to blow off their dinner date? He hoped not, but he'd understand if she was ready to call it a day. Regardless, he'd insist on stopping by the diner to pick up some food to go. She needed more than the crappy sandwiches they'd eaten earlier to replenish the energy she'd burned stressing about her grandfather.

When she closed about half the distance between them, her entire demeanor suddenly changed. It was if she'd somehow shaken off the dark cloud of worry that had been hovering over her for hours. Her smile seemed more genuine, and there was new pep in her step. Whatever had changed her mood must have been catching, because he was feeling it, too.

"Ready to escape?"

"Yeah, I most definitely am."

To prove her point, she hit the elevator button four times as if that would make it appear faster. He understood her attitude. He'd never spent a day in a hospital, but he'd visited enough friends over the years to have had his fill of the funky medicinal smells, not to mention the pall cast by years of illness and pain. As soon as they stepped outside into the cool evening air, a heavy weight slid off his shoulders. He suspected Safara felt that way, too. She paused to draw several deep breaths as if clearing her lungs.

"Do you want to ride with me or take both vehicles?"

She looped her arm through his as they headed out into the parking lot. "Why don't you follow me to the station to drop off the cruiser. Then we can go to the diner together. Afterward, you can give me a lift home. It won't be much out of your way."

Like he cared how far it was. The farther the better if it meant more time in her company. "Sounds good."

FIFTEEN MINUTES LATER found the two of them studying menus in a booth in the far back corner of the diner. Ronnie himself came over to take their orders.

"Deputy Dennell, good to see you." Then he gave Eli an assessing look and wiped his hand on his apron before holding it out. "We've haven't met. I'm Ronnie Alden, owner and chef."

The man's grip was strong and his attitude straightforward. "Eli Jervain. I'm new in the area, but I'm already a huge fan of your peach pie. I can't wait to try some of the others."

Ronnie grinned. "Hey, Safara, I like this guy."

They quickly gave him their orders and waited in companionable silence until he brought their drinks. As Eli looked around, it was obvious that most of the people scattered around the diner knew each other. Back before his life spun out of control, he might've found the curious looks sent their way amusing. Now, with everything that had happened, he wished the whole damn bunch would mind their own business.

She must have picked up on his discomfort. "They'll quit staring eventually."

"You'd think they'd never seen a stranger before."

"It's not that. A lot of strangers pass through town on their way up and down from the pass." Her eyes took on a teasing twinkle. "They're not used to seeing me having dinner with a strange man, especially a handsome one."

He liked knowing she found him attractive, but it was hard to believe she didn't have every eligible man within fifty miles hot on her trail. "Why not?"

Her pale skin flushed rosy. "I don't date much."

It was tempting to press for details, but he didn't want to make her uncomfortable. He felt obliged to share a bit of his own past. "Me, either. Too many deployments and transfers, never spending much time in any one place."

Ronnie was back with their dinners, and they concentrated on eating. It would've been a grave insult to the man's culinary skills to let the food get cold. They were on their second cup of coffee and waiting for their desserts to arrive before they started talking again.

It didn't take long to exhaust the usual casual subjects—favorite books, movies, and sports teams. Maybe it was time to move on. When he reached for the check, Safara grabbed it first. "It's my turn to buy."

"Fine, but I'm keeping score. I'll buy next time. Think if we drove to the next town, we could eat without being stared at?"

She laughed. "Maybe, but I know quite a few people there, too."

He held the door open for her. "Fine, then we'll drive even farther. Make a day of it."

And wouldn't it be great if they also made a night of it? Not that he'd suggest taking that step quite yet. Eventually, though, he wasn't going to be able to resist fanning the spark of attraction he saw in her eyes when she thought he wouldn't notice.

The evening air felt good, cool without being too cold for comfort. "How far away do you live?"

"About a mile from here on the outskirts of town. Why?"

He rocked back on his heels to stare up at the night sky. "It's a nice evening. I thought maybe we could walk."

Safara joined him in admiring the stars above. "I'd like that, but are you sure? You'll have to walk all the way back to get your truck."

"The exercise will do me good." He patted his stomach. "Especially after that giant piece of chocolate cream pie."

He let her set the pace as they strolled. Other than the

diner and the service station, all the other businesses were closed, which afforded them the closest thing they'd had to privacy all day. After the first block, he gave in to the temptation to snake his arm around her shoulders and tug her in closer to his body. He would've let go if she'd protested, but instead, she settled her left arm around his waist.

"Do you have to work tomorrow?"

Safara nodded. "No, but I'll probably go in to cover so Dad can be with my grandfather."

"I'm surprised you didn't ask your deputy friend if you could join him and his crew when they head up to my place in the morning."

She continued to walk right beside him, but there was new tension in the way she moved. They might still be physically close, but he could feel the separation anyway. "I trust Will to do it right. He's good at his job and doesn't need me looking over his shoulder. I'm sure he'll share whatever he can with Dad. Either way, it's his case, not ours."

Eli wanted to call bullshit on her, but he didn't bother. Maybe she really believed what she was saying, but more likely she hoped to throw him off the scent with her too-casual attitude. No way she or her father would be satisfied with someone else investigating her grandfather's attack. He'd bet his bottom dollar that they not only suspected the perpetrator was the same guy who had attacked Safara, but they knew it was.

If he were them, he'd go by the book and let the county sheriff's team do their job. Once Will finished his investigation up on the mountain, he'd go on the hunt himself. He'd give them twenty-four hours, forty-eight max, before Safara and maybe her father headed up to the ridge to do their own search. The only thing they wouldn't expect was for Eli to be lying in wait to see what the hell was going on up there.

But that was a problem for another day. Right now, he wanted to enjoy the last few minutes of their time together.

They turned off the main drag. "I live just down the street."

He wasn't ready to say good night and head back up the mountain by himself, but his gut instinct said this wasn't the time to press Safara for more than this quiet walk through town. There were too many secrets between them. He might wish that she'd trust him enough to tell him what was really going on, but he couldn't fault her for playing her cards close to her chest when he was doing the same thing.

"This is it."

Safara coasted to a stop in front of a small house set some distance back from the street. It was well maintained and gave off a warm and welcoming vibe.

"I'll see you to the door."

She took a step back. "You don't have to do that."

"I know. I want to."

Because he just wasn't going to walk away from her one second before absolutely necessary. She stared up at him for a long second or two and then slowly nodded. What had she seen that had her taking his hand and leading him toward her house? He couldn't find the words to ask and wasn't sure if he wanted to know the answers.

All too quickly they were standing on the porch. He waited while she dug out her keys and unlocked the door. "I don't suppose you want me to come in and look around. You know, to make sure everything is okay."

Rather than take offense, she huffed a small laugh. "While I appreciate the gentlemanly thought, I wouldn't inspire anyone with my ability to be a police officer if I'm afraid to walk into my own house by myself."

He couldn't argue with her about that. "Well, then I'll say good night, but there's one more thing I need to do before I go."

"Which is?" she asked, but from the way her dark-lashed eyes slowly drifted down to focus on his mouth, she already knew the answer.

He caught her jaw with his fingertips to tilt her head to the exact right position. "I've wanted to do this from that first night."

She lifted her hands around his neck and leaned in closer. "What were you waiting for?"

"The perfect moment."

Her eyes widened in surprise. "And you think this is it?"

"Guess we'll find out."

He brushed his lips across hers. Soft. Welcoming. Enticing. Perfect.

On the second pass, she protested. "Quit teasing."

Eli smiled and kicked the intensity up a notch. He tasted the corner of her mouth with the tip of his tongue, loving it when her lips parted long enough for her own tongue to dart out in invitation. He tightened his hold on her, pulling her flush against his chest as he deepened the kiss. She tasted like coffee with a hint of rich, dark chocolate. She was a perfect fit in his arms, her body lean and womanly. He pressed her against the door and rocked against her, letting her feel the hard evidence of how much he wanted her.

The small sounds she made drove him crazy. It was so damn tempting to carry her inside and follow this to its logical conclusion. To strip them both down to the skin and discover all of each other's secrets. To learn what she liked from a lover and then give it to her over and over again. His breath caught in his chest.

Secrets. His. Hers.

That thought dragged him back from the edge, and he banked the fire that threatened to rage out of control. He couldn't—wouldn't—take Safara to bed when he couldn't even tell her his real name. How could he ask her to trust him with her truth until he was willing to share his own? And what if those men from the crash site found him? By their choice or his own, he might have to disappear with no explanation. It wouldn't be fair to Safara to let her think they could have a future together until he could lay his past to rest.

While he waited for his pulse to slow, he tucked her head under his chin and simply held her close. "I was right. That was perfect."

He felt her smile against his chest. "No arguments there."

Time to leave. It took a surprising amount of strength to step back from the precipice. "Keep me posted on how your grandfather is doing, and thank you for dinner, not to mention the dessert."

"We both know how much you love Ronnie's pie."

"True enough," he said as he traced her smile with his fingertip. "But for the record, I wasn't talking about the pie."

Then he gave her another quick kiss, one meant to

be friendly, before walking away. He liked that she stood watching him until he was halfway down the block. She waved one last time before disappearing inside her house. He kept walking because it was the right thing to do, even if he hated every step that took him farther away from her.

THE NEXT MORNING, her father wasn't at the hospital when Safara stopped by to check on her grandfather, but her aunt arrived shortly afterward. Bitti offered to sit with Halder during the day, leaving Safara free to work. Since Jakes had spent most of the night at the hospital, he was still home in bed asleep.

Not needed at the hospital, Safara headed over to the police station. She wasn't scheduled to be out on patrol, but she could answer phones while catching up on paperwork. An hour later, she was still staring at the same report. Her mind kept wandering back to last night—or at least certain parts of it.

Eli Jervain sure knew how to kiss. If he hadn't slowed down their headlong rush, she wasn't sure she would've found the strength to step back on her own. The press of that big body against hers, rock hard in all the right places, had felt amazing. Historically, she'd always been a bit skittish when it came to sex. Letting someone get that close was not something she took lightly. It was hard enough to protect everyone caught between two worlds when she kept outsiders at arm's length. It became nearly impossible if she dropped that barrier. Most of the time it wasn't worth the effort just for a little hot sex.

Maybe it was how they'd met and everything that had happened since that made it next to impossible to maintain any distance with Eli. Admittedly, she had a thing for tall men with broad shoulders, but it was more than that. It meant something.

Or maybe she was fooling herself.

The sound of the office door opening jarred her out of the endless circle of doubts she'd been trapped in. She recognized the footsteps. Without bothering to look over her shoulder, she held up her empty mug and said, "Hi, Dad. The coffee is fresh."

She saved the still unfinished report and sat back in her chair while her father poured them each a cup and carried them over to sit down beside her desk.

"I stopped to see your grandfather on my way here. He's awake and asking when he can go home." He offered her a wry grin. "Those nurses have no idea what they're in for if they think they're going to keep him down for long."

The news that her grandfather was already stirring up trouble eased the knot of tension she'd been carrying in her heart since she'd first listened to Eli's terse phone message. "Was he able to tell you what happened?"

"A little. I didn't want to discuss it with Bitti there, and we only had a few minutes alone while she went downstairs to grab a quick bite." His expression turned grim, his gaze angry. "He was visiting a friend who lives not far from the crossing. As he was heading back to where he's been staying, he ran into Tiel's gang. Everything seemed normal until they suddenly grabbed him by the arms and dragged him into the cave."

A muscle in his jaw twitched as he spoke. "Tiel told him they wanted him to take a message back to us. Dad agreed to tell us whatever they wanted him to, but they laughed and said he *was* the message. Then they had fun cutting him up and then threw him across the barrier. I don't know if they meant to hurt Dad or kill him, but that doesn't matter. Once Will is finished with his investigation and gets his people out of our way, we'll end this threat for good."

His pronouncement wasn't a surprise, but she hated that it had come to that. The problem was tracking the culprits down. "They've obviously been slipping back and forth across at that spot for a while now."

Her father pinched the bridge of his nose as if fighting a headache. "Yeah, that's what I think, too. At least one of the bunch must be able to control the barrier. To make matters worse, I'm going to be tied up for a while taking care of your grandfather. Bitti will help out as much as she can, but she has a job and her own family to look after."

"I can help, too."

"I know, sweetheart. One way or the other, we'll manage."

They lapsed into silence for a short time. He obviously had something on his mind but was reluctant to bring it up. She had no doubt what—or actually who—the subject would be when he finally corralled his thoughts.

With a deliberate show of casual interest, he finally asked, "So, how was dinner last night?"

She wouldn't make it easy for him. She wasn't some teenager subject to her father's dictates about who she could date and who she couldn't. "Good. It was fried chicken night at the diner."

By this point, his mouth was a straight slash of frustration. "When I drove Bitti back to my house, the cruiser was parked here at the station."

She walked over to the honor bar and bought a candy bar for each of them. As she opened her own, she sat back down. "I dropped it off for one of the guys to use since I wasn't scheduled to patrol today."

"Good thinking. About Eli, did he . . . did you—"

Okay, it was time to end this discussion once and for all. "Dad, stop right there. For the last time, we are not having this conversation. What Eli and I did or did not do last night is none of your business."

Her father's hand slammed down onto her desk. "You've already made that perfectly clear. I told you my concerns about him. Now it's up to you to make the right decision."

Enough was enough. "And if my definition of 'right' doesn't match up with yours? What then, Dad?"

"Then you put all of us at risk."

She threw her candy bar across the room and lurched up to her feet. "Don't you dare lay that guilt trip on me. I've spent my entire life protecting our secrets. If you want to point fingers at the ones who'll most likely bring the Paladins down on all of our heads, then Tiel and his friends are the ones you should be talking to, not me and not Eli."

It was time to get out of there before the two of them did irreparable harm to their relationship. "It's my day off. I'm going home."

He caught up with her before she made it out of the door. "Look, I'm sorry. Maybe I was out of line."

She glared into gray eyes that matched her own.

"Seriously, Dad? Just maybe?"

"Fine. I was out of line."

That was when she realize how tired he looked. It was easy to forget all he'd been through in the past week, starting with her being attacked and then his father being almost killed. "What can I do to help?"

His shoulders slumped in relief. "Once Will and his people are done poking around up on the mountain, we need to set up a schedule of people to stand watch to figure out how often Tiel and his friends are crossing over and where they hole up when they do. Once we know that, we can organize a group to end this threat before it gets out of hand."

"Good thinking." She paused to run through her own schedule in her head. Other than work, there wasn't anything she couldn't reschedule. "I'll take first watch. When should I start?"

"Will's expecting me to call later to see what they found up there. Once he gives me the all clear, I'll let you know. But for now, plan on starting the stakeout late tomorrow afternoon or early evening."

That made sense. Oddly enough, the people from Kalithia who were afflicted with the light disease preferred to cross into this world at night. It took time for them to acclimate to the bright light of the earth's sun.

"All right. I've got a few things I need to get done if I'm going to spend tomorrow night up on the mountain."

Her father clearly wasn't happy with the situation. "I hate the idea of you up there alone, but right now I don't have anyone else I can send. Maybe I'll join you if your grandfather is doing better."

"One way or another, we'll get through this, Dad." She gave him a quick hug. "I'll park the ATV in that same spot. It's far enough from Eli's cabin that he shouldn't hear me coming. I'll skirt the clearing where he saw Tiel and me fighting. I don't want to risk drawing him into this mess any further than he already is."

"Good thinking. I'll talk to you later."

Once again she started to leave, but then turned back. "Do you ever wish we were human, Dad, and didn't have to deal with all of this? I love our people, but life would be so much simpler if we didn't have to watch every word we say. I know we came here to make sure I didn't end up like Mom, but sometimes I swear I think we should've taken our chances in Kalithia."

"Don't talk like that. Your mom wouldn't have wanted you to suffer like she did." He grimaced. "Like I did."

Like Tiel's family would when they ended his violent rampage once and for all. Her heart hurt for all of them. No one took any pleasure hunting their own kind, but this last attack left them no choice.

"I really, really hate this, Dad."

"We all do, sweetheart." Her father's smile was achingly sad as he tapped the badge on his chest. "But we took an oath to protect the people of this town."

She glanced down at her own badge and repeated the vow both he and her grandfather had said to her in the past. "It's our duty, and we'll see it done."

Even if it destroyed her soul in the process. With that happy thought, she stepped out into the sunshine and started the long walk home.

9

Eli stepped out onto the porch intending to soak up the late afternoon sunshine and read. Although not tired physically, mentally he needed some downtime after spending hours wandering around up on the ridge. Will and his crew arrived right at nine as promised, and Eli had guided them up to where he'd found Halder. Once there, Will had requested Eli stick around in case they had questions. At the same time, he was told to stay out of their way. Oh, the deputy had couched both requests in polite terms, but there was no mistaking them as anything but direct orders.

Eli had obligingly parked his ass on a handy boulder to watch the men and women set about their investigation with quiet efficiency. The one oddity in the process happened when Will had abruptly announced he'd be the only one to check out the cave.

Will had then ducked inside and stayed there for several minutes before finally reappearing. He immediately strung a spiderweb of crime scene tape across the entrance and loudly warned the others to stay out. Something about part of the ceiling in danger of collapsing or some such thing.

What was in the cave that the deputy didn't want the others to see? There hadn't been a chance to check it out with all of them watching his every move. That didn't mean he wouldn't go back on his own at some point to do a little more poking around. For now, he was going to kick back with his feet propped up on the porch railing and enjoy a cold drink and his book.

One chapter and half a beer later, he heard the soft rumble of a car engine heading his way. Who would be driving up the mountain now? Safara was his first hopeful thought, but the vehicle that he could just barely glimpse through the trees wasn't the right color for her police cruiser. Her father had no reason to come calling, and Will had said he'd call if the sheriff's department needed anything else from him. He couldn't think of anyone else local who'd make the long trek up to the cabin.

But he could think of another group that might've finally tracked him down. His boots hit the ground hard as he rolled up to his feet. He wouldn't run and hide, but neither would he face a potential threat unarmed and helpless. If he had to surrender, he'd do it on his own terms.

He hustled inside to grab his sidearm and then stepped back outside to wait. In real time, it wasn't all that long before the vehicle finally made the last turn to head directly toward the cabin. However, it felt more like the slow drag of those last few seconds between the time his team had moved into position and finally got the signal to execute their mission. He fought against the familiar rush of adrenaline pouring into his veins.

Widening his stance, he held his gun down at his side. No use in going on the offensive until he knew for sure he was about to come under attack. The big SUV rolled to a stop a short distance away. The sun glared off the tinted windshield, making it impossible to identify the driver, but at least he appeared to be alone. That didn't mean he wasn't the decoy while more men slipped into position around the cabin.

Finally the car door opened, but the driver was clearly in no hurry to leave the sanctuary of his vehicle. When he eventually did, Eli could hardly believe his eyes. He stuffed the gun into the back of his waistband and charged down the steps.

"Jamison? Is that you?"

No response. Well, shit. From his rigid stance, Eli's unexpected guest could've been a statue. Jamison hadn't changed much since he'd last seen him other than his blond hair was longer and tied back in a short ponytail, and he looked a little thinner. Back in the day, Jamison "Doc" Shaw had been the medic in Eli's unit. On their last mission together, they'd taken heavy fire while out on patrol. Jamison had pulled a wounded soldier to better cover. While he was working to control the bleeding, another insurgent got off another lucky shot and hit Doc in the leg. That bastard would never pull a trigger again, but Jamison ended up with nerve damage in his right ankle.

After extensive rehab to regain his mobility, he'd taken a medical discharge when the doctors finally told him that his slight limp was permanent. Last Eli had heard, Jamison had gone back to college to become a registered nurse.

None of that explained why he'd shown up at Martin's

cabin. How had he known he could find Eli there? The only logical answer was that he'd been in contact with Mike. He slowed his approach and waited for some sign of how his old friend was going to react to the fact Eli hadn't died in the helicopter crash.

He stopped just shy of where Doc remained frozen in the same position. "So are you going to punch me or come up on the porch and have a beer?"

If anything, the former medic looked even more angry. "I haven't decided yet, you worthless son of a bitch. I'm thinking it might take both to make me happy."

Eli edged within an arm's length. "Fair enough. All I ask is that you don't hit me in the mouth. I hate the way blood makes beer taste."

They were both of similar height, although Doc was built along leaner lines. If the situation did come to blows, it was even money on which one would come out the winner. Not that he had any intention of fighting back. He'd put all of his friends through hell by letting them think he'd died. He still wasn't sure if it wasn't better in the long run if none of them had ever found out any differently. It had only taken a couple of punches for Mike to make peace with the truth. Eli could only hope that by offering Jamison the same terms, they'd get past the anger, too.

Finally, Jamison drew back and swung straight at Eli's jaw. At the last second, he angled his fist to give him a glancing blow, one meant to sting rather than shatter bone. It still hurt like hell.

He rubbed the side of his face. "Are you done or do I have to turn the cheek and let you pound on the other side now?"

Jamison crossed his arms over his chest and glared at him. "I haven't made up my mind yet. What kind of beer do you have? If it's some off-brand cheap stuff that tastes like canned piss, I'm going to land a good one on that beak of a nose."

"Please give me credit for having good taste in something, especially when it's obvious that I suck at picking friends." He held up his fingers to count off their options. "I've got three different microbrews, all local. One is a pale ale, one is a pilsner, and the other is a nice red that I've grown quite fond of."

Jamison brushed past him on his way to the porch. He dropped into the closest chair. "Fine, start pouring while I listen to how you ended up parked on this godforsaken mountainside drinking beer. Some food wouldn't hurt, either. The major said you made a mean sandwich."

Feeling better than he had all day, Eli followed Jamison up the steps. "Fine. How long are you staying?"

"Not long. Mike sent me, but he doesn't want us to draw unwanted attention by spending too much time up here. There's no sign anyone is watching either of us, but then we might not notice if they've got the right training."

Eli pegged his friend with a hard look. "I'll tell you the same thing I told Mike. Don't put yourself at risk for me."

Jamison shrugged, clearly not worried. "Don't sweat it. We both know I'd sell you out for a six-pack and a large pizza."

Then he offered Eli a dimpled grin. "Maybe even a medium if it's the deep-dish meat-lover's special."

"Well, as long as you've got your priorities right."

Eli found himself chuckling as he threw together the

sandwiches and grabbed a couple of bottles of each type of beer, then carried them out onto the porch. After setting the tray down on the sawed-off stump that served as a table, he handed a plate to Jamison but let him pick his own beer.

They were on their second bottle when Jamison started talking. "Mike gave me the basics of what happened. It took some serious arm twisting on his part to convince me that he wasn't bullshitting me."

He glanced at Eli's hand. "He said you sliced yourself open for a bit of show-and-tell, but I don't want a repeat demonstration. Hell, if half of what he told me is true, I'm already pretty freaked out."

"Imagine how I feel."

"I'm not sure I can. But regardless, I'm glad you're not six feet under or in pieces scattered over a mountain slope somewhere." He took another long swig of his drink. "Mainly because you buy good beer. I don't want you thinking I'm getting all girly emotional about you or anything."

"That's good. I'll sleep better knowing that."

They both laughed again, which felt damn good to Eli. Before the crash, he'd had a long list of friends he could hang out with and shoot the shit. Now he had Mike and Jamison. Well, there was also Safara, but there were two major differences when it came to her. First, he still had to watch every word he said to her. Second, and most important, he had no urge to kiss either of his friends.

"So why did the major drag you into my situation at all? Not that I care, mind you."

"Mike said he thought long and hard before calling me. He figured I might not be on anyone's radar since I've been out of the army for so long. If he made too many trips up here, someone would be bound to notice if they're paying attention."

He set down his empty bottle and reached for another. "Me, I'm just a college student working part-time at a local hospital to pay the bills. I might have a beer with old friends once in a while, but mostly I'm ass deep in homework and midterms."

"That's right. I hear you're going to be a nurse."

Jamison nodded. "Yep, I plan to specialize in trauma care."

"You'll be great at it. You were the best medic we ever had."

Eli meant that. The man had balls of steel when hell came raining down and each second could mean the difference between life and death. Maybe it was time to lighten the conversation.

"So tell me this, Blondie. Are you sporting that ponytail to impress the ladies?"

Jamison offered him the one-finger salute. "No complaints so far. Besides, you're just jealous. We both know I'm not just the smart one. I'm the best looking, too."

"Asshole," Eli responded with no real heat. Rather than continue in that vein, he changed the subject. "So, you've told me why Mike picked you, but I'm guessing this was more than a social visit. If he wanted to know if I was lonely, he could've called or e-mailed me."

Jamison stood up. "I've got some papers in the car he wanted you to see. He thought about attaching them to an e-mail, but he decided to err on the side of caution. Again, we have no hard evidence that anyone is still interested in what happened to you in the crash, but we don't know they aren't, either."

Doc returned with a file folder and dropped it on Eli's lap. "Mike managed to get copies of a few pictures taken by the agencies that investigated the scene."

Eli couldn't bring himself to open the file. "I already know what the scene looked like. I was there."

And those images haunted his dreams every night in living color and surround sound. The smells, the screams, the impact—all of it. He hated the sympathy in the other man's eyes when Eli tossed the folder back to him.

"He knows that, Sarge." Jamison pulled out two eight-by-ten photos and held them up so Eli could see them. "That's not why he wanted you to see the pictures. Whoever took these shots caught a few of the men he was telling you about. He wanted to know if you recognize anybody."

Eli angled the pictures to catch the best light. Two of the men had been caught in profile. Nothing about either of them looked familiar. There was a third one who happened to look right at the camera just as the picture had been taken. Didn't look too happy about it, either. It was impossible to tell if the man's eyes were blue or gray, but they were cold as ice. A killer's eyes.

"I don't know any of these guys, but they do look like spec-ops, especially in those black uniforms."

"Mike has a few feelers out with people he trusts. He's afraid to ask too many questions for fear of stirring up a hornet's nest. If he learns more, he'll let you know, but he thought you'd be better off if you could recognize at least a few of these guys on sight."

Maybe. If they managed to track him up to the cabin, they could have the place surrounded before he had a chance to defend himself. Damn, didn't he have enough problems on his plate right now?

The sun was now riding pretty low in the sky. "As much as I've enjoyed the company, if you wait until after dark to head out, it will take you twice as long going down. Those ruts are real nut busters."

"Yeah, I was thinking the same thing." Jamison stood up and stretched. "Not sure when I'll make it back up here, but is there anything I can bring you the next time I come?"

"Just your badass self."

He followed Jamison down off the porch to where he'd parked. At the last second, his friend spun to face him. His blue eyes looked extra bright and shiny with a thin sheen of tears. He muttered a curse and then threw his arms around Eli's shoulders for a back-thumping hug.

"I'm glad you didn't get dead. I've lost enough friends. We both have."

Eli couldn't argue with that. He tried not to count the number of friends he'd lost even before the helicopter crash. "Thanks for coming."

"Yeah, well, someone's got to keep an eye on you. God knows what kind of trouble you'd get into if Mike and I didn't ride herd on your ass."

"Good luck with all that homework. Do you have a chart on the fridge that shows all the gold stars you earn?"

"Damn straight I do. My mom's so proud."

Eli was still smiling when Jamison's car drove out of sight. After gathering up the empty bottles and plates, he carried them inside and locked the door, wanting its solid strength between him and the world outside. He started to put his sidearm back into the desk drawer but changed his mind. Even if the spec-ops guys weren't lurking out there in the trees, the crazy guy with the sword might be.

After cleaning up the kitchen, he studied the array of weapons hanging on the wall. He'd always thought Martin had collected them as a hobby, but his opinion on that subject had changed. After living on the mountain for a while now, he had to wonder if Martin had wanted to make sure he could defend himself against whatever two-legged dangers lurked out in those woods.

If so, Eli knew just how he felt.

10

Safara strapped on her sword. It wasn't her first choice when it came to weapons, but she might need it if she crossed paths—and swords—with Tiel inside the cave. Bullets could shred the barrier, leaving it down for hours and adding to the danger for people on both sides of the divide.

She retrieved her gear from the back seat of her ATV. The pack contained a few necessities for standing watch up on the mountain, including the four extra boxes of ammunition that her father had insisted she take and they both hoped she wouldn't need. As ready as she'd ever be, she started the long hike up to the cave. Every few minutes, she stopped to listen, letting the normal murmurings of the mountain settle around her. So far, she was pretty sure she was alone.

That was good, although it wasn't just Tiel she was worried about. Another man wandered in these woods, and she really didn't want to cross paths with Eli right now. Well, that was a lie, especially after their kiss. Even as her head argued that it was a mistake to play with fire, other parts of her wanted to pour gas on the coals and toss in a lit match.

Or maybe a whole box of them.

That thought was not helping her ability to concentrate. She kept trudging through the trees as she gave herself a stern lecture. "Safara, keep your head in the game. Getting lost in thoughts, especially hot ones, could get you killed out here."

Besides, if she had a lick of sense, that kiss would be a onetime thing for all the usual reasons. It wouldn't be the first time she'd walked away from an attractive man because of the potential pitfalls of any long-term relationship. It made for a lot of loneliness at times, but it was the safer path to follow.

Time to take another look around. With the sun already slinking down toward the western horizon, the trees cast long shadows that made it even harder to find a clear route through the undergrowth without stumbling over rocks and roots. The path she'd taken the last time was more open, but it passed too close to Eli's cabin. Better to take the rougher trail and avoid alerting him to the fact she was back.

After cresting the last rise before the final push up to her destination, she stopped to get her bearings and start looking for the best spot to serve as her hunting blind. It had to provide a clear view of the cave entrance while at the same time affording her enough cover to avoid being seen.

She spotted a couple of likely prospects and settled on the one that offered the best view in three directions. A huge boulder roughly the size of a VW Bug would block the line of sight behind her, but then that worked both ways. Anyone coming from that direction wouldn't be able to see her, either.

She slid her backpack off her shoulders and dropped it on

the ground. Before exploring the cave for any sign of recent activity, she needed to replenish her energy. A bottle of water and an energy bar later, she drew her sword and left the sanctuary of her small hideout. She was halfway to the cave entrance, which was still covered in a web of crime scene tape, when she noticed the back of her neck was itching. It was most likely the effect of drying sweat, but what if it wasn't?

Maybe she wasn't alone on the ridge. Her grandfather was an expert on wilderness survival. Starting from when she was a young girl, he'd taught her to always pay attention to her instincts. If they said she was in danger, she most likely was. *Stop, look around, assess the situation, and then act accordingly.*

She did a slow turn to study her surroundings, not bothering to try to disguise her scrutiny. If someone was watching her, it was already too late for that. They already knew Safara was there, which left only one unanswered question. If she wasn't just being paranoid, did the eyes watching her belong to a friend or an enemy?

The simplest way to find out was to ask. She'd get an answer or she wouldn't. Either way, she would learn something about her unknown companion.

"Want to tell me why you're hanging around up here?"

Nothing but the sounds that were normal in the woods. The slight rustle of the tree branches stirring in the breeze. The call of birds in the distance. A flicker of motion as a small rodent scurried under a bush off to the left. No rush of her watcher going on the attack. She guessed that was a good thing.

Heck, maybe she was imagining things, and the sensation

was a by-product of her overstressed nerves. She resumed her march toward the cave, determined to check it out and then get back to her hideout to wait. Eventually, someone would show, even if it was only her father coming to relieve her.

She was just shy of the entrance to the cave when the interior lit up with a flash of light. Damn it, was someone coming through the barrier? She got her answer when eight Kalith—six men and two women—charged out of the cave with swords drawn. Her cousin Tiel was the last one to come into view, which told her everything she needed to know about the situation.

Raising her own sword, she injected as much authority as she could as she spoke in their native language. "Stand down! I am not here to fight unless you force the issue. Go back to Kalithia and stay there. This is not your world."

Either they didn't understand her Kalith or they didn't care what she had to say. She repeated the warning as they formed a semicircle in front of her with swords raised. Knowing she could be facing her own death, she stood her ground and said, "Fine. Let's dance."

ELI ADMITTED HE'D been a total asshole as he scrambled down the tree. He'd been sitting right above Safara's head and laughing while she'd tried to figure out where he was hiding. He had no idea what had warned her that she wasn't alone on the ridge, but it had been pretty entertaining watching her head swivel from side to side as she tried to figure out if someone was spying on her.

If he'd answered when she'd called out, he would've been down on the ground already where he could immediately join in the fight. He briefly considered staying where he was and picking off her attackers one by one with his rifle. However, with the swarm of black-clad men and women swirling around Safara, dodging in and out on the attack, he couldn't risk taking a shot for fear the bullet would go right through one of the enemy to hit Safara, too.

She was speaking in a language he didn't understand. Something with a deep, guttural sound to it, nothing like the French, Spanish, or Arabic that he spoke. Her opponents answered in kind. While he couldn't decipher the exact meaning, that they were taunting her came through loud and clear.

Out of desperation, he fired several shots over their heads, hoping to drive them back and draw their attention away from Safara. They froze for a heartbeat but then immediately renewed their attack. Cursing, he dropped the broadsword down to the ground and landed right by it. Grasping the pommel in one hand, he bellowed a challenge to the bastards who dared to attack a woman alone. Son of a bitch, was that the same guy who'd attacked Safara the other night? What the hell was going on?

"Hurt her and you die!"

For the few seconds it took him to get close to the action, he kept his eyes on Safara, her lethal grace mesmerizing. The effect on him was primal, a warrior's heart hungering for a mate whose fierce nature matched his own. She was dangerous, no mistaking that truth, but there was such beauty in the way she moved. Unfortunately, the same was true for the crazies doing their best to kill her.

So not happening, not on his watch.

He paused to fire another round of shots with his sidearm, this time closer to his targets. One of the men barked what sounded like an order. The two women backed away and took off running up and over the ridge out of sight. Eli holstered his gun and then swung his sword in a wide arc as he yelled, "Safara, I'm coming up beside you."

She spared him a quick glance. "Get back, Eli. This is my fight."

"Don't be selfish, Safara. There's enough of these bastards to go around."

Before he could stop her, she tried to slide in between him and the remaining six fighters. "Damn it, Eli, back off."

Three of the fighters had other ideas and broke away to face Eli. From that point, it got interesting. Their curved-blade swords were a blur as they came at him. He took pride in holding his own against multiple enemies, even if it was mainly due to beginners luck.

Even in the chaos of combat, there were moments of pure clarity. Who were these guys? They'd all been cut from the same mold, the similarities between them startling. Their clothing was nearly identical, varying only in the shades of gray and black in a style unlike anything he'd ever seen before. Tunics hung down to their upper thighs over close-fitting pants. Their soft-soled boots came halfway up their calves.

They all had long hair, too, which was dark with streaks of silver and dark gray despite their youthful faces. Their eyes were so pale as to be almost white. He'd seen that shade

126

of gray before, or at least close to it. Safara and her father, grandfather, and even her aunt all had eyes about that color. He'd put the similarity off to a strong family resemblance. That all of these crazies had it, too, was a coincidence he couldn't ignore.

"Eli, watch out!"

He blinked and jumped back as the tip of his closest opponent's sword came within a hairbreadth of slicing open his neck. "Son of a bitch!"

"Stand back-to-back with me."

Good thinking. At least no one would be able to come at either of them from behind that way. Regardless, he hoped like hell they could end this soon; the muscles in his arms and legs already burned with the strain of the prolonged fight.

Suddenly, other voices entered the fray as three more men charged out of the cave shouting in that same guttural language. Had they all been having a fucking party in there? This second bunch wore similar clothing to the others, but with insignias that made them look more like a uniform. They also each carried one of the same lethal blades as the other bunch. Eli's gut twisted into a knot of fear and fury, worried they were reinforcements. To his surprise—and immense relief—that wasn't the case. He didn't understand what they shouted to Safara, but she nodded and kept her attention on their original opponents. As soon as the trio moved into fighting range, the guy who had attacked Safara shouted a warning to his men about the added danger.

Thanks to the distraction, Eli wounded the guy who'd almost slit his throat, while Safara did some damage to the man closest to her. Drawing blood triggered a mass retreat of the fighters. Eli drew his gun and got off several shots before they were out of range. He thought maybe he scored one hit, but it was hard to tell once they got lost in the shadows under the trees. He started forward, prepared to follow them all the way to hell if that's what it took to end their threat for good. Safara grabbed his arm.

"Don't, Eli. There are too many of them."

He wanted to argue the point, but then another man staggered out of the cave. He was dressed in the same uniform the other three wore, and his arm hung limply at his side as if too weak to lift the weight of the sword. As soon as he appeared, the three remaining fighters retreated to stand on either side of him. They continued to hold their weapons at the ready but made no attempt to attack Eli and Safara.

The newcomer was clearly their leader. He struggled to catch his breath before he spoke, directing his words to Safara. She shook her head and said, "My companion doesn't understand our language. Speak English if you can."

He gave Eli a considering look before finally responding in English. At first, his harsh guttural accent made him difficult to understand. "You partner with a Paladin?"

Back to that again. Who the hell were these Paladins anyway? "No, I'm not a Paladin. I don't even know what that is."

The other man clearly didn't believe him, but he'd already turned his attention back to Safara. "I am Sworn Guardian Vedin s'Krom. My Blademates and I were tracking those rogues in our world. We almost had them cornered when they escaped across the barrier and then two of them working together slammed it shut again."

Pausing to press his hand against the back of his head, he then held up a bloody palm. "They disabled me first, since none of my Blademates have the power to control the barrier. It took me time to bring it down again."

Eli struggled to follow what the man was saying, and not just because of his heavy accent. What barrier was he talking about? Maybe the crime scene tape, which now hung in tatters, but that didn't explain all the strange clothing and odd weapons. No country he knew of called their soldiers Sworn Guardians, not to mention the guy talked about fighting in their world like they weren't all standing on the same piece of terra firma.

His brain hurt trying to make sense of it all, while Safara clearly understood exactly what the man was talking about. He was about to demand that she explain what was going on when Vedin's legs gave out on him. His men caught him before he hit the ground.

Safara bit her lower lip and then pulled Eli aside to whisper, "We need to get them out of sight. Can we take them to your cabin long enough to get Vedin patched up? We're all vulnerable out here right now. I also need to tell my father what's going on."

He had no reason to trust the four men, but he did trust Safara. "Fine, but then you will explain what the hell is going on here."

She swallowed hard, looking even more worried than before. "I will. I promise."

Turning back to the men in black. "Sworn Guardian, I am the granddaughter of Halder d'Ennell, daughter of Jakes d'Ennell, and sworn deputy of Ridgewick, home of many of our people. On my honor and on the blade of my family, I will see that you and your men are safe."

Vedin's eyes widened in surprise, or perhaps it was recognition. He slowly straightened and then nodded. "I, too, swear on my honor and that of my Blademates that we will accept your offer of sanctuary as allies and in friendship."

She pointed down the slope. "Eli's home is nearby. Let's go there where you can rest and tend your wounds. Once your strength has returned, we'll guide you back here. I can bring the barrier down if you need assistance."

When the other man nodded, she pointed in the direction of Eli's cabin. "Start walking toward those trees, and we will catch up with you shortly. I need to show my friend something first."

Her gaze swung back toward Eli. "My companion has never seen what lies in the back of that cave. It is time he does."

Vedin didn't look happy, but he didn't argue. Instead, he said something to his men, who spread out across the small clearing and drew their weapons. By way of explanation, the warrior said, "Better that we stand watch to make sure our enemies don't return."

Safara merely nodded and headed toward the cave. Eli managed to hold his tongue until they reached the entrance. When he was reasonably sure they were out of hearing, he wheeled around to glare down at Safara. "Start talking, and don't hold anything back."

"I need to show you something first."

She took his hand, her palm warm against his as she led him into the cave. The light outside didn't penetrate very far beyond the entrance, but she moved through the darkness with confidence. She stopped right about where he remembered the cave bending around to the left.

"Eli, you've guessed I've been hiding the truth from you about the attacks on both me and my grandfather. This cave is one of those things. I have no right to ask it of you, but promise you will to keep our secrets. Lives depend on it."

"I don't make promises when I'm shooting blind, Safara. The best I can offer is to listen to everything you have to say before I make a decision one way or the other."

She must have realized that was as good as she was going to get under the circumstances, because she led him those last few steps down the passage. Odd that it was less dark even though they'd come some distance from the entrance. Another turn made the reason for that blazingly clear. The entire back wall of the cave was a shimmering wall of light. It was so bright that he had to blink several times to give his eyes the chance to adjust. Then he watched in stunned amazement as various hues swirled into sight and then just as quickly faded away only to be replaced by another splash of color.

It was beautiful and yet terrifying. He released his death grip on Safara's hand and edged closer, the strange compulsion to reach out and touch it almost impossible to resist. She immediately caught his arm and jerked it back.

"Watch it, Eli. That barrier has enough voltage to fry your brain."

Now that she mentioned it, he could feel the buzz vibrating deep in his bones. He'd never seen the likes of it, yet it felt oddly familiar to him as if it spoke to him on some level.

"Are there more of these things around? Where did it come from?"

Because if this barrier had always been there, wouldn't someone have talked about it? If not on the news, then in some kind of nature special on television?

Safara remained close by him, her pretty face awash with the flickering colors of the barrier. "Yes, there are more pieces of the barrier scattered around the world, mostly in areas like this one where the tectonic plates meet up. As to how they formed in the first place, I have no idea. I don't think anyone does."

"So you and your family aren't the only ones who know about this?"

She crossed her arms over her chest with a shiver that he doubted had anything to do with the chilly temperature of the cave. "No, we're not, although we try hard to keep outsiders from finding out about them."

"And I'm an outsider?" For some reason that pissed him off big-time.

A slow nod was her only answer. After a few seconds, she drew a slow breath. "I'm going to show you one more thing before we go. Stand back a little."

When he was in position, she slowly raised her hands out toward the barrier, palms forward, and began to chant. He couldn't understand the words, but they had the same cadence as the language she'd been speaking with the Sworn Guardian earlier. As her voice grew stronger, the light in the barrier grew thinner bit by bit until it flickered and disappeared altogether.

The cave extended across the line where the barrier had been seconds before. He started forward, but Safara remained where she was. "Aren't you coming?"

She shook her head, sweat beading up on her skin as if she were under a strain. "No, and you can't stay over there very long. The exit is just beyond those boulders. Poke your head out of the cave carefully and make sure no one sees you. If it's safe, take a good look around, especially up at the sky, and then hustle right back. I can't keep the barrier down for long, and we can't risk you being trapped over there."

He did as she told him. Outside the entrance, the terrain was completely different from where they'd entered the cave on the other side. The low rolling hills were covered in scrub vegetation, more like what grew in the high desert of Eastern Washington, and nothing at all like the towering Douglas firs and cedars he was used to. And the sky was a dull gray and completely devoid of clouds. How was this all possible? He noticed he was breathing hard as if he'd been running, his lungs struggling to fill with oxygen. Was it shock or thin air? So many questions.

"Time's up, Eli. Come back."

He scanned the distant horizon one last time before turning his back on all the strangeness. As soon as he rejoined Safara, she resumed chanting. Within seconds, the barrier returned, colors swirling and buzzing away. From the way her shoulders slumped, the process had taken a lot out of her.

"Are you okay?"

She nodded. "We need to get back to Vedin and the others. Let me catch my breath before you start the inquisition."

"Just one question before we go." He pointed back

toward the barrier. "Where is that place? Because it's sure not anywhere on this mountainside."

"That much is true, Eli." Safara paused to stare up at him, her worried eyes taking his measure. "In fact, it's not even on this planet. Now let's get out of here."

Then she walked away, leaving him staring at the barrier. Was she really expecting him to believe that he'd just stepped foot in another world?

The answer was obvious—yeah, she did. It was hard to argue with the little demonstration she'd just provided him. In less than thirty yards, he'd gone from the lush, green terrain of the Pacific Northwest to a high desert. The plant life was unfamiliar, and the sky was a strange color. Hell, even the air smelled different and felt thinner.

So either she was crazy or he was for believing her. Only one way to find out which of those two things was true. He'd listen to what she had to say and go from there.

He made his way toward the entrance of the cave, the one right there on planet Earth. Along the way, he wondered what his life was coming to when the best outcome from today's events would be to learn he'd lost not just his life in that helicopter crash, but his mind as well.

11

Her father was going to have a full-on hissy fit when he found out what she'd just done, but surely he'd realize why she'd had to introduce Eli to their reality. Then again, maybe not. He'd made his opinion on her involvement with Eli all too clear. Regardless, it was too late now.

Her thoughts spun in circles as she left the cool interior of the cave behind. She crossed the clearing to point Vedin and his men in the direction of Eli's cabin, promising to join them shortly. She stopped long enough to retrieve her backpack, not because she particularly needed it right then. It was more of an excuse to wait for Eli. If he didn't reappear soon, she'd have to go back in after him.

He finally stepped out of the cave, his hard gaze immediately zeroing in on her. He pointed toward a large tree off to the side of the clearing. "I have to go back up to get my gear, then I'll catch up with you."

She smiled for the first time in what felt like forever. "So, sneaky man, that's where you were hiding."

He set his sword down on the ground and then grinned

back at her as he started to climb, standing on a boulder to boost himself up to the lowest branch. "Yeah. Most people don't think to look up."

"Well, I will from now on."

She hurried over to stand underneath the spreading branches of the tree to check out where he'd been hiding. Not all that high up, but enough that he wouldn't be easily seen by anyone approaching on the ground.

"Here, make yourself useful."

The unexpected demand left her with barely enough time to get her hands up to catch his backpack. She set it aside but kept her eyes focused on the limbs above her head in case something else came flying her way. A second later, Eli dropped down from his perch with a rifle slung over his shoulder.

"We'd better get a move on. Wouldn't want your alien invaders to get lost. Can you imagine trying to explain them to the search-and-rescue people?"

She knew he was trying to lighten the mood, but the crack about alien invaders struck a little too close to home. "You do realize that I'm one of those aliens, too."

He didn't look all that shocked. "Yeah, I've put a few of the pieces together. It would help if I knew what the rest of the puzzle looked like."

He pointed toward the trees. "Vedin and his buddies didn't make it very far."

The Sworn Guardian was sitting on a log with his three Blademates surrounding him, their hands on the pommels of their swords. He slowly stood back up as they approached. "We weren't sure where to go from here."

Eli pointed toward the next rise. "My place is about a ten-minute hike from here in that direction."

Then he frowned. "Okay, I'm not sure if you know what a minute is, but it won't take us long to get there. Do you need help walking?"

Vedin tilted his head to the side to acknowledge the offer of assistance. "No, I should be able to get that far."

Eli took the other man at his word. "Safara, lead the way while I guard the rear."

He turned back to Vedin. "Give a holler if you need her to slow down."

Normally, she might've protested the way he was issuing orders right and left, but it was interesting to see this side of him. Even while he spoke, his eyes were constantly on the move, watching their surroundings for any sign of danger. Clearly he was used to being in command in any similar situation. He'd also assumed responsibility not only for her safety, but for the Kalith warriors as well. She had no doubt at all that he wouldn't hesitate to put himself between all of them and any perceived threat. His military background was definitely on display right now, and he was in full warrior mode.

It was sexy as hell.

Rather than follow that thought down the rabbit hole, she walked past the Sworn Guardian and his men. "This way, gentlemen."

The six of them walked through the trees and gathering darkness in near silence. Vedin was breathing hard, but he kept up with the pace she'd set. She stopped at the edge of the trees overlooking Eli's home. All was quiet.

He moved up beside her and leaned down to speak close to her ear. "I have some problems of my own, so let me go ahead. I'll flash the lights twice if it's safe to approach. If I don't give the all clear within five minutes, hightail it out of here and call your father for help."

What problems? She started to protest, "But—"

"I mean it, Safara. You don't need to get tangled up in my mess on top of everything else you're dealing with right now. Promise you'll do as I say."

She wanted to refuse, but once again her unconditional loyalty to her people kicked in. She couldn't put Vedin and his men at further risk. "Fine, but don't expect me to be happy about it."

His grin shone brightly in the shadows. "I won't."

Then he brushed his lips across hers before disappearing back into the trees. He was all but invisible as he circled around to approach the cabin from the other side. That made sense. If anyone was watching, he'd draw their attention away from where she and her companions stood waiting.

Each of the Kalith males gave her an odd look and then turned to stare toward the trees where Eli had gone. Maybe they didn't approve of a Kalith woman letting a human man kiss her. She might have her own misgivings on the subject, but it was her decision to make. She flexed her hand on the pommel of her sword. If any of them dared to voice an opinion on the subject, she'd set them straight big-time.

Speaking of Eli, how long had he been gone? It seemed like forever, but it couldn't have been more than three, maybe four minutes. Finally, the lights in the kitchen window flickered on and off twice before coming back on to stay.

"All right, it's safe to go now."

The five of them moved out single file, still keeping a wary eye on their surroundings. Eli opened the front door just as she stepped up on the porch. He looked past her to Vedin. "Come in and have a seat."

His intense gaze switched back to her. "While I patch up your friend, would you mind seeing what kind of food you can scrounge for us?"

Okay, that might be a problem. "Vedin, do you and your men ever eat meat?"

From the look that flashed across Eli's face, it was obvious that he was a hard-core carnivore. Her people tended to be vegetarian, but mainly because meat was so hard to come by in Kalithia. It was hard not to snicker, but she didn't want to insult either him or their guests. From the slight smile on Vedin's face, she suspected he had also noticed Eli's response. "We will eat whatever you can provide and be grateful for it."

"I'll see what I can do."

While she rooted through the kitchen cabinets and the refrigerator to come up with enough to feed six people, Eli made quick work of cleaning the wound on the back of Vedin's head. The Kalith warrior then stripped off his tunic to allow easy access to the gash on his right forearm, which revealed his well-muscled torso. Wow, the man was totally ripped. When Eli caught her watching, he frowned. He immediately ducked back down the hall and returned with a short-sleeved T-shirt for Vedin to wear. Maybe he thought it would keep the Kalith warrior warm, but she suspected he didn't much like the guy flashing all those muscles around her.

Cute.

After wiping away the dried blood, Eli studied the wound on Vedin's arm. "These butterfly bandages should be enough. I've stitched a few wounds in my time, but that hurts like hell. I'll leave the choice up to you."

Vedin nodded in the direction of the bandages Eli had held up. "Those should be fine. My gift of healing is a minor one, but this wound will be almost gone by tomorrow this time."

Eli jerked as if he'd been shocked. What was that all about? He immediately schooled his features, which she took to mean he wouldn't want her to ask him right now. Later, though, she'd find some way to bring up the subject. She turned her attention back to their makeshift meal while he finished wrapping Vedin's arm with gauze and surgical tape.

"The food is ready. Come serve yourselves."

She waited until the five men filed over to the counter before speaking again. "I heated up two kinds of soup—chicken noodle and vegetable beef. You can make your own sandwiches. You have a choice of ham, salami, turkey, and two kinds of cheese."

Vedin translated her explanation for his men, who evidently didn't speak English, or at least not enough to easily follow what she'd said.

Even then, they waited and watched while Eli made his way along the lineup, filling his plate and soup bowl as he went. Once they were all settled at the table, she fixed her own plate and joined them.

Despite the simple fare, the four Kalith warriors seemed to enjoy the meal. No one seemed inclined to do much talking, which was fine with her. She had a difficult conversation ahead of her once the Sworn Guardian and his men returned home. As if sensing the direction her thoughts had gone, Eli looked up. He seemed remarkably calm for a man whose entire view of reality had just been radically altered.

He finished the last bite of his sandwich and sat back. "Do you guys feel up to returning home tonight, or do you need to crash on my living room floor?"

The puzzled look on Vedin's face as he tried to figure out what Eli was asking him was pretty funny. The idioms in English were often a puzzle to the Kalith no matter how fluent they were in the language.

She did her best to explain. "He's asking if you want to sleep on his floor rather than hike back up to cross the barrier tonight."

Eli laughed. "I'm sorry. I didn't realize how that sounded. Crashing in this case means to stay somewhere unexpectedly."

"Thank you both for the explanations and the kind offer." Vedin paused to speak to his men before continuing. "We should return home as soon as possible. I need to report the attack on us to our Guildmaster and alert him that the rogues have become more active in this area. He will need to increase patrols near the cave on our side of the barrier."

Eli carried his empty plate and bowl over to the counter near the sink. "Let me know when you're ready to leave."

While she and Eli made quick work of the cleanup, she noticed Vedin's men had gathered around the impressive array of weapons on the wall. They clearly found the various blades fascinating. One started to touch a rapier, but Vedin barked an order that had the man jerking his hand back down to his side.

Eli joined them in front of the display. "It's all right. Feel free to handle any of the weapons you find interesting."

He took the rapier down and offered it to the Blademate who'd shown interest in it. "I don't know where he got all of these, but most of them have been hanging on this wall since before I was born."

Once again Vedin played translator. In short order, they took down several swords and even a double-bladed ax to examine closely, which made Safara smile. Evidently boys love their toys no matter which side of the barrier they were born on.

"Hey, while you guys do that, I need to call my father." Which was another conversation she wasn't looking forward to at all. "It shouldn't take long."

Eli handed Vedin the machete he'd been holding and joined her near the door. "I'm guessing he won't be thrilled to find out that I stumbled into all of this. Do you want me to talk to him instead?"

"Thanks, but he'll want to hear it from me, since he was supposed to take over for me at some point. I also need to see how Granddad is doing."

She stepped out onto the porch and dialed her father's number. He answered on the second ring. "Hi, I expected you to check in before this. What's going on up there?"

Safara hadn't gotten very far with her explanation when her father interrupted her, his anger coming through all too clearly when he said, "What happened to our plan of waiting and watching?"

She didn't blame him for being upset. Facing off against eight rogues by herself wasn't the smartest thing she'd ever done. If she'd been in her hiding spot when they came charging out of the cave, she would've stayed there. Probably.

"Remember, I wasn't alone. Eli was there, too. We were holding our own when Vedin's Blademates showed up. The rogues broke off fighting and ran away. One funny thing, though. The Sworn Guardian assumed Eli was a Paladin, just like I did when I first met him."

Her father didn't let himself get distracted. "Son of a bitch! And what was Eli doing there in the first place? Didn't I warn you about letting him poke his nose in our business?"

Sometimes her father forgot that her temper matched his. "So you'd rather I'd have died on a Kalith sword than for Eli to learn the truth?"

A sharp intake of breath was followed by a slow sigh. "Safara, you know better that that, but it's hard enough to keep a lid on things without dragging outsiders into the situation."

And there was the real problem. Eli wasn't an outsider, not anymore. Time to change the subject for a minute. "How is Granddad doing?"

"Not all that good. He was a lousy patient to begin with, and then he started running a slight fever. They upped the antibiotics and gave him something to knock back his pain. Personally, I think they should give me some of that, too. You know, to take the edge off the pain the old man causes me with his nonstop complaining."

She laughed. "The problem is the two of you are so much alike."

He didn't bother to deny it. "True enough. Your aunt went back home, so I'm stuck babysitting the old coot for the foreseeable future. I won't make it up there tonight, although I hate to leave it all on your shoulders. Of course, since Tiel is already on our side of the barrier, there's not much use in watching the cave entrance. If they cross back over, hopefully that Sworn Guardian and his men will be waiting for them."

Them trying to return to Kalithia wasn't her real worry. "If it is the light disease driving all of them across the barrier, what if Tiel and the others go on the attack? Tiel alone was bad enough. If they're running in a pack, there's no telling what will happen."

"There's nothing we can do about that until we figure out where they're headed. I'll alert our contacts in the area. If they hear or see anything, they'll let us know."

That was true, but was it enough? She hesitated, knowing he wasn't going to like her next question. "Dad, do you think we should notify the Paladins in Seattle to see if they can send in some support?"

It wasn't the first time she'd brought up that subject, but old-timers like her father and grandfather couldn't get past their hatred for the age-old enemies of their people. On some level, she understood how they felt. After all, her own mother had died on a Paladin sword. There wasn't a Kalith in this world or their own who didn't have the same kind of horror story to tell about a loved one.

But her logical mind never failed to point out that the Paladins fought a never-ending battle to protect this world from a malignant invasion. Most of the time, the people who crossed the barrier from Kalithia were sick, driven by a need to kill anyone who crossed their path. Maybe if the Kalith people did more to keep their problem people from escaping into this world, the Paladins could become allies instead of enemies. The only time she'd dared to say that in front of her grandfather, he'd gone ballistic. It had been tempting to remind him about the old saying that if they kept doing the same thing over and over, they'd always get the same result.

Her father finally answered. "You know that's not going to happen, Safara. If those bastards somehow tracked the message back to us, we'd all end up getting shoved back into Kalithia permanently. I'd probably be fine, but you can't risk it."

She hated the pain in his voice when he added, "I can't lose you like I did her."

Although she didn't remember her mother, she'd never for one moment doubted that she'd been the love of her father's life. "All right, Dad, but you know I had to ask. I have enough leave coming to take tomorrow and the next day off if necessary. I'll stay up here until you or someone else comes to relieve me."

The door behind her creaked as Eli stepped out on the porch. He leaned against the railing next to her but remained silent until she disconnected the call. "I take it he's not happy. Is it because of your grandfather or because of me?"

No use in sugarcoating the situation. "Both, not to mention the situation with Vedin and his Blademates and the men they were chasing." She nodded toward the door. "Are they ready to go home?"

"Yes. They're anxious to get back and sound the alarm."

She rested her head against Eli's shoulder, drawing strength from the contact. "I suppose you're wanting that explanation I promised."

He pressed a soft kiss to her forehead. "It can wait until we take these guys home, and you get some rest."

"Thanks."

Before he called Vedin and the others to come outside, she stopped him. "Tell me, Eli. How badly freaked out are you by all of this?"

His smile was a little bit sad. "Honey, as far as reasons to freak out go, I have personal experience with ones far worse. Remind me to tell you about it sometime."

Maybe she'd finally find out what put those shadows in his eyes and why a man like him was living off the grid in this remote cabin. "I'll do that."

Five minutes later, their small parade headed back up the mountain toward the cave.

12

Did the barrier ever get less fascinating? Maybe. For sure, no one else seemed to pay it any special notice. With some effort Eli managed to drag his attention back to his companions. The Sworn Guardian and Safara were quietly chatting in Vedin's native language, most likely for the benefit of his Blademates. He didn't mind being left out of the conversation, at least not much. Besides, it was only fair. Vedin's men hadn't been able to understand much of anything that had been said since they'd first stumbled out of the cave.

Safara ended the conversation with a slow nod as if he'd said something of great import to her. Afterward, Vedin walked over to Eli. "We are grateful for your hospitality and inviting us to crash."

His words were accompanied by a small smile, but then his expression turned serious. "You also may call upon my sword if ever you have need of it."

It was hard to know what to say to the unexpected offer, but Eli did his best to respond in kind. "Uh, thank you, Sworn

Guardian. I offer you my blade as well."

Then he patted his sidearm. "And my gun, which would probably do you more good considering my lack of experience with a sword."

Vedin responded to that last part with another of his quick smiles. Eli didn't know if the people in the other world shook hands, but he held his out anyway. Vedin clasped his forearm instead, so he did the same. To his surprise, all three of the Blademates followed suit before they lined up across the cave facing the barrier.

Meanwhile, Safara positioned herself next to the Sworn Guardian, and they both raised their hands with their palms facing the barrier. She did all the chanting, but Vedin's face was also showing definite signs of strain. The barrier immediately started to dim, finally disappearing with a crackling snap. For the second time, Eli tried to get his head around the fact that he was looking into another world. Fucking amazing.

Meanwhile, the aliens hustled their asses back across the line. They turned back to face him and Safara. Vedin stood in the middle with two of his Blademates at his side and one behind him. The four men bowed their heads slightly and then stood at attention until Safara released her hold on the barrier. When it reappeared, sparkling in all its beauty, she took a step back looking pale and breathing hard.

Eli closed the distance between them to put his arm around her shoulders. "That takes a lot out of you, doesn't it?"

"Yeah, it does." She brushed her hair back from her face. "It's usually easier when there are two of us working to bring it down, but Vedin wasn't up to full strength."

He was pretty sure he already knew the answer to his next question. "And not everyone can do that, right? Like me, for instance."

"The gift tends to run in families. My dad's mother had it, but my grandfather doesn't. That's why I was up here on the mountain that first night. He'd been on the other side visiting some friends, and I was checking to see if he was ready to come home. When I brought the barrier down, it was my cousin Tiel waiting on the other side. You already know how that turned out."

That rat bastard was her cousin? Before he could figure out what to say about that, he noticed she was shivering. "Let's get out of here. It's a little warmer outside, not to mention I don't want to be trapped in here if Tiel and his buddies suddenly get homesick."

"Good thinking."

"Let me go first." Figuring she might argue, he immediately drew his weapon just in case and started walking back in the direction of the entrance.

Safara didn't try to stop him, probably proof of how tired she really was. That didn't keep her from commenting on his high-handed behavior. "You do know that I'm a highly trained law officer. I've been protecting myself for years now."

Should he remind her that she'd hauled her delectable ass up on this mountain twice since he'd known her only to end up in a sword fight each time? She'd survived the first instance because he'd come running when she screamed. This most recent escapade would've ended in a much different way if Vedin and his men hadn't charged to their rescue. Yeah, he and Safara might've thinned out the ranks of the enemy, but the truth remained that they had been outnumbered four to one.

When they stepped out of the cave, she planted herself right in front of him. "Eli, you do know that, don't you?"

He'd really hoped she'd let it go, but she was nothing if not stubborn. "Yes, I know you're a deputy, Safara. I trust you can handle yourself in the course of your job, but even cops are vulnerable to attack."

Pointing back at the cave, he let some of his anger come boiling out. "But tonight you could've been killed if I hadn't been up in that tree. No, make that you *would* have been killed."

She met him glare for glare. "You don't know that."

"Honey, I've been in enough firefights to know the odds were stacked against you. God knows you're hell on wheels with that fancy sword of yours, but eight to one are bad odds by anyone's definition."

"But—"

He cut off her protest. "I've lost enough friends recently, Safara. I don't want to bury any more. I can't, and especially not you."

She flinched as if his words wounded her in some way. Her hand briefly settled against his chest right over his heart before dropping back down to her side. "I don't want to hurt you, Eli, but I won't ignore my duty to my people. It's not in me to do so. If you can't live with that, then there's no future for us. Not even friendship."

He wanted to back away, to protect himself from further loss, but his bullheaded size thirteens refused to take that first step. "Fine, but just know I'll want some reasonable concessions from you when it comes to all this barrier stuff. Got that?"

"I seem to remember someone recently saying he didn't make promises until he knew all the facts. Who could that have been?" She poked his chest with her finger. "Oh yeah, that was you. That seems like a good policy to me."

Eli captured her hand with his and held on tight. "Fine. Here's the deal. Whenever possible, I want to know in advance when you're coming up here. Otherwise, I'm going to have to build myself a comfortable platform up in that damn tree."

"Agreed, although I can't promise that I can give you a lot of notice."

"And I want to know the full story of what is going on. I've spent years keeping my mouth shut about the missions the army sent me on. If my word was good enough for Uncle Sam, it should be good enough for you and your father."

"Agreed, only because I'd already decided to tell you everything I can."

Okay, was she trying to hedge her bets? That was not happening.

"Not everything you can, Safara. Everything, period."

She was already shaking her head. "I won't leave out anything that would endanger your life, and I won't tell you any lies. However, there are people who have worked hard to pass as human in this world. I won't out them all just to satisfy your curiosity. It wouldn't be fair to them."

As much as he might not like it, she had a point. Besides, he had his own new identity to protect. He wouldn't appreciate it if Mike or Jamison decided to start blabbing his secrets to some stranger no matter how much they trusted the person.

"It's a deal."

A dark shadow washed over them, drawing his attention up to the sky overhead. Clouds were rolling in, and there was a damp scent in the air. "We'll continue this discussion back at the cabin, because it's going to start pouring any minute now."

Then he frowned. "Unless you were planning on heading back down to your place tonight."

"No, especially if you don't mind me crashing on your couch again." She grinned, probably in memory of Vedin's confusion over that expression. "I'd like to hang around and keep an eye out for that group of rogues."

This was sounding better and better. "My house is your house."

Especially if he could coax her into sharing his bed instead of camping out in the living room. Now wasn't the time for that discussion, not with the first fat drops of rain splattering down from above.

By the time they'd made the short hike back to the cabin, they were both soaked to the bone. That didn't mean he was going to lead her straight to the front door without first doing another perimeter check. He couldn't risk leading her into a trap.

"Wait here. I'll flash the lights again."

She took shelter under the low branches of a nearby cedar. "Fine, but you've got some explaining to do, too."

The last thing he wanted to do was drag her into his problems. Regardless, she had to know the risks of getting further involved with him. "I will."

It seemed reasonable to seal the promise with a kiss or, hell, that was probably just an excuse for what he wanted to do anyway. In his defense, he really meant to keep it simple, but he should've known better. There was nothing simple about his reaction to the sweet and spicy taste of Safara Dennell.

If she had resisted, if she'd protested at all, he would've stepped back, flashed her a quick grin to keep matters light, and disappeared into the trees to make sure there weren't any bogeymen lurking out there in the darkness. She didn't do any of that as her hands slid up around his neck, making him a willing prisoner within the circle of her arms. She was the one who deepened the kiss, her lips and tongue taking no prisoners.

The world around them disappeared from his consciousness, probably not a smart thing under the circumstances. He couldn't bring himself to give a damn. Who could worry about commandos or crazies when he had this warm and willing woman in his arms? Not him, that was for damn sure.

He stroked Safara's back, loving her supple strength and wishing it was her bare skin he was touching instead of the cotton fabric of her uniform shirt. His hands had moved on south to palm her lush backside when the breeze suddenly kicked up. Evidently the branches overhead had been storing up cold rainwater for just such a moment and proceeded to dump the entire load on the two of them.

Safara squealed and jumped back as the blast of cold hit them. At least, he thought she was the one who made that noise. He hoped she was, anyway, because Special Forces guys didn't do such things. He tried to swipe the dripping water off his face with the hem of his shirt, but it was too wet to be of much help.

"Let's get inside. I'll flash the signal as soon as I circle around to the other side of the cabin."

She nodded as she tried to wring what looked to be a gallon of water from her hair. "Fine, but hurry. I'm freezing out here."

He gave her a quick hug followed by an even quicker kiss. When she started to protest, he said, "I'm just marking my spot. I wouldn't want to lose track of where I was."

She was still sputtering when he took off at a slow lope through the trees.

THAT MAN WAS going to be the death of her. There were still rogues running loose in the woods, not to mention it was pouring outside. Any sensible person would already be inside with the doors locked and a roaring blaze in the fireplace. But she never felt at all sensible when she was with Eli Jervain.

Even now, her body vibrated from the intensity of that kiss. If that tree hadn't decided to give them both an icy shower, there was no telling how out of control things would've gotten. She wasn't the type of woman who fantasized about being taken hard and fast by a green-eyed warrior up against a tree. At least she didn't used to be. However, the minute those big hands of his settled on her ass, she was ready to wrap her legs around his hips and hope he'd take the hint.

The lights blinked on and off. It was about time. Her teeth

were chattering, and without Eli there to keep her warm, her body had turned into a giant Popsicle. She nearly stumbled going up the steps to the porch, but Eli was there to steady her. He handed her a towel as he led her inside.

"You can have the shower first."

She wasn't going to argue. She also wasn't going to invite him to join her, as tempting as that thought might be. One of them had to show some common sense. The further they traveled along this path, the harder it would be to turn back. If they ever did take that final step . . . no, *when* they did take that final step, she didn't want a bunch of secrets between them. Especially because this would never be about hot sex with no expectations. She wanted more from him, something more for the both of them.

"You okay?"

How long had she been standing there lost in the possibilities? She immediately knelt to unlace her boots, using that as an excuse to avoid meeting Eli's gaze for fear her expression might reveal the hunger she felt for his touch.

When she stood back up, he held out his hands. "I'll take your boots and put them with mine over by the fire. There are clean towels in the linen closet. I laid out the toothbrush you used the last time and that same set of sweats."

He offered her a quick grin. "Sorry I don't have any suspenders to help you keep the pants up. I could cut you a length of rope for a belt. That would make quite a fashion statement."

"Smart-ass."

There went another killer smile. "True enough. But if you play your cards right, by which I mean taking a fast shower so there's enough hot water left for me, I'll have a mug of hot chocolate waiting when you get out."

"It's a deal."

"Good. When you get done, put your wet things on the washer in the utility room. I'll run them through later, so you have something dry to wear in the morning."

"Thanks, I appreciate it."

She picked up the backpack she'd left in the cabin earlier and headed down the hall to make good on her promise to hurry. The water was hot enough to sting her goose-bumpy skin and warmed her up quickly. By the time she dried off and put on Eli's oversized sweats and socks, she felt a whole lot better. Wrapping her wet hair in a towel, she went in search of her host.

Eli looked up from where he was sitting at the kitchen table when she came back into the room. "I'm impressed. I expected that to take a lot longer."

"I figured my hair would dry faster if I sat by the fire to brush it." She tossed her pack aside and started rubbing her hair with the towel. "Besides, you'd be surprised what I can be motivated to do with the promise of chocolate."

He headed over to the stove to fill a mug. After tossing in some mini marshmallows, he set it on the table. "Thanks for the heads-up. I'll definitely keep that in mind for future reference."

The gleam in his eyes left little doubt that he was thinking about what else he'd like to motivate her to do. She sipped her drink. The rich chocolate and that seductive gaze chased the last remnants of the night's chill from her skin, leaving her all warm and toasty, not to mention tempted by the man standing within arm's reach.

He knew it, too. Eli shuffled half a step toward her and then abruptly stopped. His hungry expression slowly morphed into something that looked more like regret. "Safara, honey, don't doubt I want this. Hell, I want you so damn much it hurts, but we still haven't had that talk. For your sake, I think that should come first."

They both knew he was right. That didn't mean either of them had to like it.

"Go take your shower. I'll be waiting when you get out."

He looked so relieved that she had to wonder if he really thought she'd chicken out and take off to avoid having that discussion they kept promising to have. Worse yet, did he want her to? She didn't think she'd misread him that badly, but it wouldn't hurt to ask. "I told Dad I might stay up here on the mountain for the next day or two. Maybe I should've asked you if that was okay first."

"Of course it's okay. I want you here. Damn, I'm screwing this up, aren't I? I don't mean to." He ran his fingers through his still wet hair, looking frustrated. "You matter to me, Safara. I want to get whatever this is between us right."

"Me, too."

"Okay, then. I'll be back in a few."

Once again, he dove in closer to give her another one of his hit-and-run kisses. Then, just as quickly, he was gone. Staring down the empty hallway, she smiled and touched her lips. That man really knew how to kiss. While she waited for him to return, she sat on the raised hearth to soak up the heat and brush the tangles out of her hair.

A few strokes later, a stray thought had her smiling.

As much as she enjoyed the flickering warmth of the fire, it was a poor substitute for generating a whole different kind of heat with Eli.

When the door down the hall opened, she kept right on brushing her hair, needing to focus on something other than the man prowling toward her. When he appeared at the edge of her peripheral vision, she tightened her grip on the brush.

"The other world is called Kalithia, and its sun is dying."

Eli parked himself on the other end of the hearth. "Well, that's a problem."

She offered him a snarky smile. "You think?"

He held up his hands in apology. "Sorry. I didn't mean to interrupt."

"Apology accepted, and I shouldn't be so touchy. This is hard for me to talk about." She set the brush down and picked up the threads of her narrative. "It's been going on for forever, I guess, and the people there have adapted as best they can. Most are vegetarian, not by choice but by necessity. It's too expensive and difficult to raise animals just for meat. Power is hard to come by, too, so they lack a lot of the technology that you take for granted in this world."

Eli slid closer to her, his strong arm once again anchoring her to his side. "So that's why your people try to cross over to this world."

All right, here came the ugly part. "It's why some of us come over, but it's not true for everyone. There's an illness that some Kalith are susceptible to. I don't know if there is a more technical name for it, but we call it the light disease. As far as we can tell, it's the increasing lack of bright sunshine that triggers it. When someone succumbs to the illness, they crave the light and will do anything to find it. Once that happens, he or she is no longer the person they used to be. They grow violent and have no conscience."

It didn't take long for Eli to put some of the pieces together for himself. "Your cousin and those other rogues—they have it."

She nodded. "Yes, and it tends to run in families. My mother died of the disease, which is why my father and grandfather risked everything to bring me into this world to live. They were afraid that I would come down with it, too."

"So it's terminal?"

She wasn't sure if the sympathy in his voice made it easier or harder to continue, but she'd promised to lay it all out for him, and she would.

"Not in the way you mean. What happens is what you've already seen with Tiel. They find a way to cross the barrier into this world. Most of the time, they are out of their heads and ready to kill."

For the first time, Eli looked skeptical. "It can't be easy to keep something like that out of the headlines. I've spent a lot of time out of the country the past few years on various deployments, but I think I would've still heard if sword-wielding whackos were running around the countryside."

Wincing at his harsh description, she continued. "Fortunately, not all that many Kalith have the gift to control the barrier that Vedin and I have. Additionally, there are huge swaths of the world that don't have any pieces of the barrier at all. They're mainly located in areas where tectonic plates come together. A lot are in the Ring of Fire around the Pacific Ocean. Others are near major fault lines like the New

Madrid in the Midwest."

Time to explain the role Paladins played in this whole thing and see if Eli figured out why both she and Vedin had mistaken him for one. "Regardless, this isn't a recent development. According to our history, it has been going on forever. At some point in the distant past, a class of specialized fighters called the Paladins took on defending the known stretches of the barrier in this world. Now, a group known simply as the Regents oversees the Paladins, making sure they have everything they need to do the job."

She shot him a quick look. "I've never personally met one, but I can tell you what I learned about the Paladins from people who have. They are all big men, most over six feet tall. Depending on who you talk to or maybe which side of the barrier you were born on, they are considered either cold-blooded killers or else highly trained warriors."

Talking was thirsty work, but she kept up the explanation while she walked over to the fridge to fetch them each a beer. "Paladins fight with bladed weapons, mostly swords. I'm guessing they're equally good with firearms, but it's not safe to use bullets near the barrier. They tear holes in it that are hard to repair. It's not good for anyone if the barrier stays down for any length of time. And since the stretches of barrier are usually in caves, ricochets can be a real problem. The Paladins guard the barrier, defending this world against the Kalith trying to cross over. I understand they call us Others, not Kalith. I guess it's easier to kill people who have no real identity. And, to be fair, they're not really wrong about that."

She tried really hard not to picture her mother as one of those people. "You see, the Kalith they cross swords with are all sick with the light disease. By the time they encounter the Paladins, they are out of their minds with bloodlust. They're no longer the people they used to be. To give credit where it's due, the Paladins do try to force them back into Kalithia. But failing that, they'll slaughter them to prevent them from going on a rampage in this world."

"And that's how your mother died?"

She really didn't want to discuss it, so she just nodded and kept going. "There are never enough Paladins to go around, but at least they are really hard to kill. Remember that gift for healing that Vedin mentioned? Well, the Paladins have that ability, but on steroids. By all reports, there's almost nothing that will kill them, and even if it does, they don't stay that way."

She held out Eli's drink, but he didn't seem to even see it. There was no telling where his head was right now, but it wasn't with her. She had more to tell him, but maybe he needed a minute to absorb everything she'd already said. When the silence dragged on for another couple of minutes, she nudged him with her shoulder.

"Are you okay?"

He blinked a couple of times and then shook his head as if to clear it. "Any idea where these guys come from? I mean, are they Kalith like Vedin or are they human?"

"As far as I know, they originated here on Earth, but I've heard they have a few Kalith genes mixed in with their human DNA. It only stands to reason that some Kalith have managed to blend into this world. If they married humans along the way, their children would've inherited some Kalith traits and passed them down through the generations. I've always figured that's where Paladins got the ability to heal like they do. Rumor has it that they also live longer than normal humans do. Kalith people often live well past a hundred years. The bad news is that the Paladins can only come back from death so many times before they go crazy just like the Kalith who develop the light disease."

By this point, Eli was frowning big-time. "I noticed your family and Vedin's bunch all have unusually pale gray eyes. I didn't think anything about your father and aunt having salt-and-pepper hair considering their age. But Vedin and his men have it, too, even though they look like young men. Are those common Kalith traits?"

She nodded as she fingered a lock of her hair. "I've been dyeing my hair since my early teens to hide the gray. A lot of my people also wear colored contacts to blend in better with the human population."

"Are the same things true of the Paladins?"

Something about the way he asked made her think he wasn't simply being curious. "As far as I know, Paladins don't have a specific type when it comes to looks or coloring. Why?"

Eli lapsed into another long silence. He shifted positions so his elbows rested on his knees as he stared across at the weapons on the wall. The flickering of the flames outlined the grim set to his jaw. Whatever he was thinking wasn't good. She thought he'd known and accepted that she wasn't human. From the way he'd kissed her earlier, she'd been convinced that didn't matter to him, but maybe she'd been wrong about that.

"Eli, this was a lot to throw at you all at once. I'm sorry to have dragged you into my world. It was bound to freak you out a bit."

Well, actually a whole lot, from the way he was acting. Her heart ached at the possibility that all of this was proving to be too much for him to accept. When she started to get up, he caught her arm and tugged her back down beside him. "It's not you, Safara. It's me."

"What about you?" Not that she really wanted to know, when the expression in his eyes was so bleak it hurt to look at them.

"You're not the only one who has been living a lie. I'm not Martin's distant relative. I'm his grandson, and my legal name is Master Sergeant Eli Yates."

Now he was the one not making much sense. "But you said his grandson died in a helicopter crash. Dad even checked to see that was true. He said everyone was killed on impact."

Eli shuddered. "We were."

Then his mouth curved up in a travesty of a smile. "Lucky me. I'm the only one who didn't stay that way."

"But if you came back from death, then that means—"

She stopped, unable to say the words out loud. Unfortunately, Eli had no such hesitation and finished the sentence for her. "My best guess, I'm genetically one of those Paladins your family hates so much. Congratulations, you and Vedin were both right even if you were only guessing."

She started to deny it, but what was the point? Ignoring it wouldn't change the truth of the situation. "It must have come from Martin's side of the family. But no one ever said anything about the Paladins or having a Kalith ancestor?"

"Looking back, Martin must have known something. The

last time I saw him, he went ballistic when I told him I'd enlisted. He went on a crazy rant about not risking the truth coming out and not staying dead."

He glanced down at her with a frown. "I probably shouldn't ask this, but do you know how to put me in contact with a Paladin? Seems like that's the only way I'll get answers to my questions."

Now she was the one shivering. "No, I don't. My father might have some idea, but I can pretty much guarantee he won't tell you. It would be too risky for everyone else if you were to draw their attention in this direction."

Eli straightened up and put his arm around her shoulders again. "I can't blame him for feeling that way. It's not only his job, it's his family he's protecting. I'll just have to figure out how to reach out to the Paladins without them being able to trace me back here. If that's not possible, I'll move. I never planned to stay here permanently."

She hated the thought of Eli leaving, even if it would be best for the safety of all concerned. Her father might've eventually come to accept her getting involved with a human man rather than one of the Kalith males who lived in this world. But he'd never accept a Paladin, the enemy of their people and the kind of man who had killed her mother.

The room went blurry. "We are so screwed."

Eli brushed away the tears trickling down her cheeks with his fingers. "Yeah, that pretty much sums it up."

"So what are we going to do?"

"This."

He kissed her hard, as if driven by the knowledge their time was running out. She hated that he wasn't wrong about that. With that in mind, she kissed him back. After all, they still had tonight.

13

He had no business kissing Safara right now, or maybe ever, but at the moment Eli didn't give a damn about right and wrong. He'd just told her his worst secret, and while there were others he hadn't yet revealed, at least she hadn't run screaming out the door.

He wrapped Safara in his arms on his lap, holding her close without crushing her. If she wanted to break free of the embrace, she could so without much of a struggle. He owed her that much. He'd let her go if she suddenly decided she didn't want his Paladin hands on her sweet body. For the moment, he'd enjoy playing tongue tag with her even if having her sitting right on his erection was driving him crazy.

She suddenly broke off the kiss, her breathing ragged as she stared up at him with those pretty gray eyes. "Are you all right with this? Even if it can only be for tonight?"

Was she crazy? Even with most of his blood supply pooled below his waist, he was smart enough not to ask that question. "There are two worlds out there, but they can take care of themselves for the next few hours. Right now their problems don't involve us."

As soon as he spoke, she shifted her position so she was straddling his thighs. "That's good thinking. There's just us and our own little world."

She punctuated her words with a series of kisses along his jawline. As her fingertips followed the same path, he realized he hadn't bothered to shave. Too late now, but at least he could apologize.

"Sorry if my whiskers are too rough."

"I like it. Feels good against my skin." To prove her point, she rubbed her cheek against his. Laughing softly, she added, "It tickles."

He hoped she felt that way when he got around to kissing some of her more sensitive bits and pieces. For now, he slipped one hand under the hem of the sweatshirt he'd loaned her. Tracing the curve of her spine up to her shoulders and then back down, he noted she wasn't wearing a bra. That discovery inspired him to do a little more exploring. At the first touch of his hand against the fullness of her breast, Safara leaned into his palm, murmuring her approval as she rocked against the rock-solid proof of how much he was enjoying it himself.

There were too many layers of clothing between them. Grabbing the hem of her shirt, he peeled it up and over her head. The glow of the fire painted her skin in shades of gold and peach. Beautiful. He caught her nipple with his lips and teased it into a stiff peak with quick flicks of his tongue and then gentle pressure with his teeth.

"Eli," she sighed.

He paid equal homage to her other breast, loving the taste of her warm skin on his tongue. Safara grew more frantic and began trying to strip off his shirt. The minute his bare chest came into contact with hers, his control shattered. He was up off the hearth with an armload of gorgeous woman. She wrapped her legs around his waist and her arms around his neck.

It was tempting to lay her down on the floor in front of the fire, but she deserved better than that. He'd make it as far as the bedroom if it killed him. Light spilled in from the hall to illuminate the bed, guiding his way. He tumbled them both down on the king-sized mattress, twisting at the last second so that he landed on his back with Safara sprawled across his chest.

She pushed herself up into a sitting position, still straddling his lap. "Nice move, big guy. Now, where shall I start?"

"Any damn place you want to." He clasped his hands under his head to see what she had in mind. Safara arched over his chest to nibble on his chin and then kissed her way down the side of his neck to where it joined his shoulder. From there, she slid farther down his body, using both her fingernails and her tongue to explore his chest.

He admired the fullness of her breasts as she moved over him, wanting more than anything to fill his hands with their warm weight. He'd get around to it, but right now he wasn't about to interrupt her determined journey down his body. Not if she was headed where he hoped she was. Prayed she was.

Oh God, she was. She nuzzled his erection through the heavy thickness of his fleece sweats. His back arched up off the mattress hard enough to almost toss her off. Safara gave him a smug smile. "Liked that, did you?"

He flexed his hips in an unsubtle hint for more of the same. "I'd think that would be obvious."

When she hooked her fingers in his elastic waistband, he lifted his hips so she could tug his sweats down several inches. Not nearly low enough as far as he was concerned, but she looked awfully pleased with what she'd uncovered so far. Her fingers settled around his cock in a firm grip as she lifted it up to meet her lips. When she kissed the tip, his brain imploded.

Time to take control of the situation. With a lightning fast move, he grabbed her arms and flipped Safara over onto her back. He smothered her protest with an openmouthed kiss and used one of his legs to anchor hers right where he wanted them. Following her example, he kissed his way down to her nipples, stopping long enough to suckle each of them in turn. From there, he traced the lower curves of her breasts before exploring her belly button with the tip of his tongue.

She wiggled and protested, "That tickles!"

Making note of that fact for later use, he moved onward and downward. His sweats were so loose on her that they practically slid down past her hips on their own as she moved and twisted in response to his kisses. He sat up long enough to pull them down the length of her long legs and threw them someplace over his shoulder. His own followed, removing the last barrier between them.

The scent of her arousal filled his senses as he positioned himself between her legs, spreading them wide. He brushed his fingers through the curls at the junction of her thighs. "I want to taste you, Safara. Are you ready for that?"

Her pale eyes widened when she realized his intent. He waited until she nodded before resuming the soft strokes, gently parting her folds before finally using his tongue to continue his explorations. She made low noises of pleasure as her fingers tangled in his hair, holding him right where he most wanted to be.

"So damn sweet."

It didn't take long before she arched up off the bed as she rode out her climax. As the tension flowed out of her body, he kissed her one last time and then moved back up to cover her body with his. "Give me a minute, and we'll see if we can top that."

Her smile held a lot of satisfaction. "I'm not sure that's possible."

"We in the Special Forces love a challenge." Not that he was still part of that elite group, but he wasn't going to let that dampen his good mood.

"Okay, soldier, let's see what you've got."

Moving to sit on the edge of the bed, he opened the box of condoms he'd bought on his last trip to town. A few seconds later, he stretched out beside Safara on the bed, ready to show her another good time.

"Now, where did I leave off?"

"I bet you can figure it out. But just in case, here's a hint."

With her eyes at half-mast, she smiled as her fingertips traced a meandering path down between her breasts before continuing down the length of her torso. His cock jerked in reaction as if it had been his body she'd been stroking rather than her own. When she held her arms up in invitation, he didn't hesitate. The time for slow and easy was past. He needed to possess this woman, to claim her fast and hard, to show her without words that this mattered to him. How much she mattered to him.

Settling his body over hers, he supported most of his weight on his elbows as he rocked against the entrance of her body. "Better brace yourself, babe. I'm not sure how long I can keep this slow and easy."

"I'm okay with that." Then she settled her hands on his rib cage and dug her nails in just enough to sting. "Kiss me first."

A soldier knew how to follow orders. His kissed her a long time, using his tongue to offer a preview of the dance they were about to start. He flexed his hips and then pushed forward, repeating the steps until their bodies were joined. Feeling her tense at the invasion, he prayed for the strength to remain frozen in position long enough for her body to adjust.

When she finally let out a slow breath, he withdrew a short distance and slowly pressed forward again. She took his length more easily this time. After a third thrust, she was right there with him demanding everything he could give her. He kicked it into high gear, pulling her legs higher up around his hips as he set a pounding rhythm. Their sweat-slicked bodies slid against each other with a delicious friction that had both of them breathing hard and straining toward their common objective.

Safara pushed at his shoulders. "My turn."

He obligingly rolled over onto his back and let her take control. It took her a few seconds to establish a tempo. She rode him slow and easy, but that was okay. He liked watching the gentle sway of her breasts as she moved forward and back. He palmed them with a soft squeeze. Murmuring her approval, she leaned into his hands, increasing the pleasure for them both.

Gradually, her movements picked up speed and grew more frantic. He settled his hands on her hips to steady her as he thrust upward, deep and hard, and no holding back. For this one instant, she was his, the connection between them powerful and complete. Her voice rang out so damn sweetly when another climax hit her. The pulsing of her inner muscles shoved him straight over the edge with her. After they rode out the last few waves of heated pleasure together, she collapsed in a boneless heap on his chest.

Nuzzling her neck, he whispered, "Pretty damn good for our first time."

"Yeah, it was." He felt her smile against his chest. "Can't wait to see what the second round looks like."

"If it's much better than that, I'm not sure I'll survive it."

She lifted her gaze to meet his. "Not a problem. As I recall, if it kills you, you won't stay that way. And once you're back to breathing again, we can go for round three."

He never thought he'd find anything about his freaky nature funny, but he was grateful to her for making him laugh about it at least this once. And to show his gratitude, he poured everything he had into round two.

TIME HAD NO meaning in the dark comfort of Eli's bed. Safara could've lain there next to him for an eternity and never grown tired of being comforted by his powerful body and gentle touches. Unfortunately, the sun would soon rise over the mountain, and their first night together would have to end. Until it did, though, she wasn't going to waste a single second on sleep.

"You're thinking too hard. It's keeping me awake."

Eli's deep voice was a grumbly rumble right next to her ear, his breath a warm flutter against her skin. They were lying spooned together, his arm over her waist and holding her flush against his chest. Neither of them had bothered putting on any of their scattered clothing, partially because it would take too much effort to hunt it all down, but mainly they'd just have to take it all off again the next time they made love.

And from the impressive pressure against her backside right now, that time might be any minute now. "Well, maybe I could do something to take the edge off so you can get back to sleep."

She pressed back against him and wiggled a little to get his attention. "I think this would be round four. Are you up for it?"

"I think the answer to that is pretty obvious." He caught her hand and pressed it against some pretty hard evidence. Then he laughed and reached for the box on the bedside table. "Besides, who's counting?"

"Not me."

Sunrise would come when it would. Until it did, she lost herself in her lover's kiss.

BREAKFAST WAS A joint effort. She made fresh blueberry muffins while Eli cooked the bacon and scrambled a skillet full of eggs. The rain had moved on during the night, leaving the sky overhead clear. They decided to eat out on the porch where the air was fragrant with the damp scent of cedar and firs.

It had seemed like too much food for two people, but they managed to eat most of it. Thanks to last night's activities, they'd both worked up bigger than normal appetites. When they were done, Eli carried the dishes back inside and returned with a second cup of coffee for each of them. For a short time, they were content to sip the rich brew and enjoy the quiet sounds of the surrounding woods.

Safara didn't know about Eli, but she was reluctant to break the silence. The last thing she wanted right now was for the outside worlds to intrude on this special time they were sharing. They couldn't ignore their problems for long, but she'd be grateful for every minute of peace they got.

Unfortunately, Eli's cell phone started ringing. He stared at it for a few seconds before finally sliding his finger over the screen to accept the call. As he did so, he stood up and turned his back to her. Whoever was calling clearly was cause for alarm. Considering his body language, it wouldn't hurt to offer him a little privacy. She picked up both coffee cups and headed back into the cabin.

The sound of his voice carried even through the thick cabin walls. Although she couldn't make out the specific words, the tone was all too clear. He sounded angry or maybe concerned. While she waited for him to finish, she poured another cup of coffee and then started washing the dishes. The door opened just as she set the last one in the drainer. Eli usually let the dishes dry on their own, but she needed something to keep her hands busy. Picking up a towel, she began wiping a plate.

"Is everything okay?"

"Not exactly. We're about to get company. Two friends of mine, guys I served with in the army."

She set the dish towel aside and turned to face him. "Do they know what happened? You know, in the helicopter crash?"

Because she could only imagine how those conversations would've gone. Then it occurred to her to ask, "Does this mean you're considered AWOL from the army?"

His expression turned even more grim. "I will be if the powers that be ever figure out that I survived. As far as I know, the official word is that I died in the crash."

Something was definitely off about what he'd just said, maybe in the way he said it. "And the unofficial word?"

"From what I hear, the jury might be still out on that, which is why I need to explain a few things before my friends get here." He checked his watch. "Which will be in about fifteen minutes."

She took a seat at the table. "I'm listening."

14

Where to start? Not all the way back at the beginning of this mess. She already knew he'd died in the crash, a fact that hadn't rattled her nearly as much as it had him. Still did, in fact. But then she'd grown up knowing such a thing was possible. He'd never even heard of the Paladins, much less that he might've come out of the same gene pool. At least he now had an explanation for his freaky ability to heal.

"I take it you trust these men."

He spun a chair around backward and straddled it, his arms crossed on the back. "With my life. With yours, too, for that matter."

Her eyebrows sank low over her eyes at that comment. "You're not going to tell them everything I've told you, Eli. You can't."

And there was the problem. How did he tell Mike and Jamison about what he'd learned about his weird DNA without telling them where it had come from? "Your truth has become so twisted up with mine that it will be hard to separate it all out."

176

She slammed her hands down on the table. "Damn it, you promised, Eli."

Maybe not in so many words, but that didn't mean anything. Not after last night. They might not have a future together, but he wouldn't dishonor what they did have with a betrayal. He met her angry gaze head-on but kept his voice low and even. "You have my word that I will do my damnedest to keep your people out of the line of fire, Safara. My friends don't need to know anything about Kalithia, the rogues, or the truth about your people who live in our world."

She slowly nodded as most of the tension drained out of her posture. "So what are you going to tell them?"

"That depends on why they're coming up here. Major Mike Voss was . . . is my commanding officer. He was the first one to find out I was still alive. He figured I might need someone else I could contact if things go to hell in a handcart and thought Jamison Shaw would be a good choice. Doc was the medic in our unit until he left the service a while back to go to nursing school. He shouldn't be on anyone's radar. Some of my other friends might be."

"Just whose radar is Mike worried about?"

He couldn't risk dragging her into his problems when she already had so much on her own plate, but she should be forewarned. "Mike didn't know that last time he and I talked. He sent Jamison up here to show me pictures of some guys. They were poking around the crash site and asking a bunch of questions, but they weren't part of the usual alphabet soup agencies that investigate that sort of thing."

Safara got up to top off her coffee. "Why would he assume they were interested in you?"

"Nothing specific, but Mike's got a top-notch bullshit detector. If he sensed something was off about those guys, I believe him. Afterward, he came up to Martin's cabin, hoping to locate someone who might have known me." He couldn't help but laugh. "You should've seen the look on his face when he found me instead."

He rubbed his jaw in memory of that particular conversation. "I slashed my hand open to convince him that I was telling him the truth about what happened."

She looked horrified. "Did you have to do that for Jamison, too?"

He chuckled. "No, but it was a close thing. Mike had already told him about it, and Doc kept staring at my hand whenever he thought I wouldn't notice."

"How are you going to explain me being here?"

"Good question." He gave the matter some thought. "It might be safer for you if we tell them you were here for professional reasons. You know, stick as close to the truth as possible and play the deputy card. Tell them your grandfather was attacked up here on the mountain and that I found him. You needed to ask me some follow-up questions."

"And how do we explain how I got here without my patrol car?"

Good point. "You left your vehicle where the attack happened and then hiked your sexy ass over here."

Her cheeks flushed a bit rosy at his comment, but she looked pleased with his assessment. "Okay, but maybe I'd better put on my uniform."

She headed down the hall toward the bathroom. Good thinking on her part. Meanwhile, he did a quick survey of the cabin to see if there was anything else that might cause them problems.

The dish drainer held two of everything. He shoved the clean dishes back into the cabinets, and then headed for the bedroom. The sheets and blankets were a twisted mess, not to mention the empty foil packets scattered on the bedside table. He gathered them up and stuck them into his pocket to toss in the trash under the kitchen sink. It didn't take him long to put the bed to rights even though he hated erasing all evidence of the amazing night they'd shared. Of course, if Safara followed her original intentions of staying up on the mountain until tomorrow, maybe they could have a repeat performance. A man could always hope.

She followed him into the room. "Oh man, you're fast. I was just coming in here to make the bed myself."

He pulled her close for a quick kiss. "After Mike and Jamison leave, we can have fun messing it up again. You know, just so you can have a turn straightening things up."

She patted him on the cheek. "Wow, the sacrifices you're willing to make. What a guy."

The sound of a big fist pounding on the front door cut their conversation short. "I'm guessing your friends are here."

"Their timing always did suck."

She followed him back down the hall, stopping him before he reached the front door. "So are we going to go with me being up here for professional reasons only?"

He considered that option but finally rejected it. "On second thought, no. That might be why you're here today, but these guys are great at reading body language. If we try to convince them that we're not even friends, they're going to think we're hiding something."

Which they were.

She looked doubtful but didn't argue. "I'll follow your lead."

When the knocking started again, he yelled, "Hold your horses. I'm coming."

He yanked the door open to find Jamison standing there with his fist ready to start another round of pounding.

"What took you so long, Sarge?"

Then he spotted Safara and stumbled back a step, his gaze ping-ponging between her and Eli. "Uh, Major, Sarge has company of the female persuasion. We should come back later."

Mike joined him on the porch. "If this is a bad time . . ."

"No, it's fine." Eli stepped back and opened the door wider. "Come on in."

Once his friends filed inside, he performed the necessary introductions. "Major Mike Voss, Jamison 'Doc' Shaw, this is Deputy Safara Dennell from down in Ridgewick."

Safara offered her hand to each man in turn. "It's nice to meet you."

Mike kept it quick and professional. "Same here, Deputy."

In contrast, Jamison held on to her hand a little longer. "So, Deputy Dennell, what kind of trouble is our boy in? Do we need to arrange for bail? 'Cause I'm not sure we'll be able to scrape up the money anytime soon."

Then the jerk flashed his dimples that always attracted more than his fair share of women over the years. "Maybe the two of us can negotiate a better deal for him over dinner sometime."

Eli considered punching his friend, but Safara only rolled her eyes at Jamison's heavy-handed flirting. "Sorry to disappoint, Doc, but he isn't in trouble."

She glanced at Eli and then continued. "I stopped by to follow up on an incident that happened a couple of days ago. My grandfather was assaulted by persons unknown while he was hiking. Eli found Granddad and got him to the hospital down in Ridgewick just in time. Otherwise, we might've lost him."

There was no mistaking the very real emotion in her voice. "I came to let him know Granddad is expected to make a full recovery, all thanks to him. The county sheriff's department is handling the investigation, but I wanted to take a look around the site where it happened for myself."

Mike glanced at Eli as he said, "We're sorry to hear about your grandfather. I'm glad he's going to be okay."

Jamison nodded in agreement and added, "Your grandfather is lucky that it was Sarge who found him. Eli here has a real talent for saving people's asses. I can't tell you how many in our unit owe their lives to him."

Eli appreciated the sentiment, but he didn't deserve it. Not anymore. He sure as hell hadn't done a damn thing for Montez and the others who died in the crash. Yeah, he didn't crash the helicopter, but he still carried a shitload of guilt for walking away when they didn't. He couldn't imagine a time when the memory of their deaths would fade, when it wouldn't still stab like a knife to his heart.

That was a worry for another day. Right now, he needed to figure out what was going on with Mike and Doc. It might not have been obvious to someone who didn't know them well, but they were far more worried about what had happened to Safara's grandfather than they should be. It wasn't like they actually knew Halder.

"You guys park it on the couch while I make some coffee for everybody."

Safara stopped him. "Why don't I do that? I'm sure the three of you have a lot to talk about. While it's brewing, I can check in with my office."

"Okay. The coffee is in the canister on the counter, and the mugs are in the cabinet to the left of the sink."

She headed for the kitchen, calling back over her shoulder, "I'll manage as long as you don't mind me rooting around to find what I need."

"No problem."

Meanwhile, Mike was edging toward the door. "It's a nice day out, Eli, and I've spent too many hours shut up in the car with Doc. Can we sit out on the porch?"

"Sure thing. Give me a minute, and I'll be right out."

He'd noticed that both men looked a bit ragged around the edges. He wasn't surprised that Doc was still sporting his ponytail, but he didn't usually look like he'd slept in his clothes. Normally, the major looked pretty spit-and-polished even in civvies, but he hadn't shaved and had dark circles under his eyes.

After his friends disappeared out onto the porch, Eli joined Safara in the kitchen. "I don't know what's going on with them, but it doesn't look good. Can you give us a few minutes alone?"

She filled the reservoir on the coffeemaker. "Not a problem. I really do need to call Dad. Now's as good a time as any."

He checked to make sure Mike and Doc weren't peeking in the windows to see what was taking him so long. Then he wrapped his arms around Safara from behind, pulling her back against his chest. Nuzzling the side of her neck, he said, "I'm sorry they interrupted our morning, but I can't imagine that they'll stay long."

She angled her head to the side as she measured out the coffee, which he took to mean that she liked what he was doing and wanted more of it. He nibbled his way down the curve of her neck. When he teased the shell of her ear with the tip of his tongue, she shivered.

"Better stop that before they come looking for you. Take as long with them as you need. When it's safe to come out, stick your head in the door and ask when the coffee will be ready or if I need help carrying it out. Meanwhile, take the extra muffins for them to munch on."

He kissed her one last time. "Yes, ma'am, will do. And thanks for being so understanding."

When he joined Mike and Doc on the porch, they both gave him the evil eye. Leave it to Doc to be the one to start the interrogation. "So how long have you and the lovely lady of the law been, um, friends?"

"Since right after I moved up here to the mountain."

No use in telling them how that meeting came about. If they found out he'd charged to her rescue armed with nothing but a broadsword, they'd never let him hear the end of it. "I asked her if she could check into how Grandpa Martin died, although I told her he was a distant relative. She got a copy of the report from the county sheriff's office for me."

Mike reached for one of the muffins. "So was she curious about why a distant relative had moved into Martin's cabin instead of his grandson?"

"I told her about the helicopter crash. If she did any checking into my story, the facts would confirm Eli Yates was part of the crew that died that day."

Damn, he hated lying to his friends, even in a small way. At least they seemed to buy what he was selling. "So what happened that brought you both up here today? I thought we were going to keep in-person contact to a minimum."

Doc gave the door a pointed look. "Do we have time to talk before Safara rejoins us?"

"Yeah, she needed to call her father, who's the chief of police in town. He's at the hospital with her grandfather."

Mike frowned. "About the old man. Do you think he was attacked by the guys who might be hunting you?"

Eli couldn't tell them the truth about who was behind the attack, but he could reassure them that it had nothing to do with him. "No way. Whoever attacked Halder did a sloppy job of it. The men you saw at the crash site have no reason to go after Halder, but regardless it would have been a clean kill."

"That's good. Well, not that he got attacked, but that it was someone else." Mike drew a deep breath and launched into his explanation. "I got a call from an army buddy who works in personnel back east. He wanted to know what I'd done to garner the attention of some super-secret group whose headquarters is located in a distant corner of the base. They came in asking about me and one of my men who'd gone missing recently. He said these guys are black ops for sure, the kind where no one knows who they report to or who holds their leashes. They must have a helluva operating budget, because they have all the cool toys."

Mike's eyebrows rode low over his eyes. "When he pushed back, he got told pretty damn quickly that smart people pretended the bastards were invisible, but he didn't much like the idea of my name being bandied about without me knowing about it."

Eli cut loose with a string of curses that had Jamison grinning in appreciation of his creativity. "Damn, Sarge, you must have been practicing."

"Screw you, Doc," he said with no real heat. All of his anger was aimed at the men who might prove to be a threat to all of his friends. Turning his attention back to Mike, he reiterated what he'd told him the first time he'd come up to the cabin. "Throw me under the bus if something like this happens again."

Mike had obviously honed his own ability to string together colorful expressions. Jamison almost choked on his muffin. Laughing, he sputtered, "God, Major, I don't think some of that is physically possible."

Eli could only agree. "And even it if were possible, it would be damn painful."

"Can the crap, both of you." Mike gave them both a disgusted look before zeroing in on Eli. "Do not presume to insult me or my honor like that again, Sergeant. I wouldn't turn you over to those bastards even if it means I spend the rest of my military career behind bars."

"So what do you suggest I do? I don't want to live

constantly having to look over my shoulder."

In fact, what he really wanted was his life back, but that wasn't going to happen. It was also time to share a little of what he'd learned from Safara with his friends, but without outing her or her people.

"I may have some idea why they're suspicious about what happened that day. It could be something as simple as them not finding enough physical evidence to verify I died in the explosion. But I think it's something more than that."

He held up the hand he'd slashed open to remind Mike how quickly his body could repair itself. "I've been doing some research, and I suspect I'm not the only one who has this ability to heal. So far I've only found vague hints, but no hard data. I will keep digging until I do. These guys could be hunting not just me, but others like me."

Mike looked doubtful. "But how would they know? Granted, you're a total badass, especially when under fire, but Special Forces is chock-full of men like that. There's nothing about you that stands out in a crowd. And it's not like you have a tattoo on your forehead announcing your ability to the world."

Jamison gave Eli a considering look. "You could carry some kind of marker in your blood. Maybe a particular gene sequence. If your DNA is otherwise close to normal, the sequence wouldn't stand out unless someone was specifically looking for it."

Mike stalked to the far end of the porch to stare at the snow-peaked mountains in the distance. "No one is supposed to have access to the military DNA records unless that's the only way to determine someone's identity."

Eli joined him at the railing. "Yeah, that's true, but these guys don't play by normal rules. If someone figured out there were people out there who could come back from otherwise lethal wounds, it would only make sense that they'd want to recruit them for the worst missions."

Jamison followed them, his slight limp more evident than usual. "They'd also want to find out how it all works. You know, in case it's something they could use to create some kind of super soldier."

He clapped Eli on the shoulder. "I hope I'm wrong about that, but I wouldn't count on it."

"Don't sweat it, Doc. It's nothing I haven't thought about myself. Even when my head was still ringing from the explosion, I knew there was no way I could explain surviving when no one else did. I did toss pieces of my bloody BDUs into the fire, hoping they'd find enough of my DNA in the fabric to assume I'd been killed. Maybe that was a mistake."

Mike shook his head. "No way to know for sure what triggered their interest. Maybe they keep an eye out for any anomalies when someone is injured or dies in combat. If there are others with your ability, you might not be the first one to have popped up on their radar."

First or not, how could he defend himself against an enemy with no name and with no obvious agenda?

"Any suggestions about what I should do?"

Mike turned to lean against the railing. "You mean short of turning yourself in, don't you? Because if you're thinking that would be the simple answer, think again. If they get their hands on you, there's no telling where you'll end up or what they'll do. You might never see the light of day again."

Eli wanted to punch something. They were just spinning their wheels now. Meanwhile, Safara had to be wondering what was taking them so long.

"Why don't you guys sit down while I check on the coffee?"

Doc headed for the chairs, but Mike hung back. "I brought each of us a burner phone. I want you to call one of us daily. If we don't hear from you, we'll come running."

"Make it every other day. I don't always get reception up here, and I don't get to town every day."

"Fine, but if one of us doesn't hear from you for seventy-two hours, don't let it be because you forgot to check in. I'd have to do some serious ass kicking."

"Seriously? Why would I forget?"

Mike's smile turned sly. "Maybe because you and the lovely Safara picked up where you left off before we got here this morning, which could definitely cause a man to lose his train of thought."

Damn, he thought they'd put up a better front than that. "What gave us away?"

His friend laughed. "Nothing, but you just did. I wondered if you would admit it if my suspicions were on target. I'm happy for you."

"Yeah, well, don't get too carried away. I'm not exactly in a position for happily-ever-afters, and Safara has her own reasons for not wanting anything beyond the short term."

Mike crossed his arms over his chest and shook his head in disbelief. "I've gotta tell you, Eli, you don't look at her like she's just a good time on a weekend pass."

What could he say to that? If he denied the truth of Mike's

words, he'd end up lying to his friend and himself while insulting the special connection between him and Safara.

"Go take a load off. I'll go see what's keeping the coffee."

"Sorry I brought it up."

"Don't be. Someone should know that the two of us are involved. If those guys come after me, she could get caught in the crossfire. If you don't hear from me, promise you or Doc will check to make sure she's all right. I'll send you both her contact information."

The major's shoulders snapped back as if he were standing at attention. "You have my word on that, Sergeant."

It would've seemed weird to salute when they were both out of uniform. Instead, he held out his hand and said, "Thank you, sir."

Mike's stance softened just a hair. "I'd do the same for any of my men, Eli. You might not be on active duty right now, but our bond goes deeper than the uniforms we wear."

Which was why Eli wouldn't hesitate to lay his life down for this man and so many others like him with whom he'd served. When battles raged and lives were on the line, a soldier fought for those who served side by side with him. That kind of loyalty couldn't be bought; it had to be earned.

"I'll go get that coffee now."

"I like cream and sugar in mine. And Sleeping Beauty over there will take his any way you want to give it to him, preferably cold and full of grounds. After we drink it, we'll head back down to civilization."

Then his friend smiled and wandered back over to where Jamison sat dozing with his feet up on the railing and his baseball cap pulled down low over his eyes. As Eli headed inside, Mike started giving Doc hell for sleeping on the job, a little taste of normalcy in a world that had gone crazy.

15

Where had the time gone? Yesterday, Mike and Doc had hung around with her and Eli until after lunch before finally heading back home. It had been fun watching the three men taking potshots at each other with stories laced with good humor and insults. She envied the depth of their friendship. Thanks to both her job and her ancestry, Safara knew very few people with whom she could drop her guard and let it all hang out.

Trust normally came slow to her, yet Eli had somehow crashed through all of her carefully constructed protections to take up residence in her heart and her bed. Well, technically, she'd ended up in his bed, but even that was out of character for her. That wasn't to say she had regrets about her impulsive behavior other than how bad it was going to hurt to walk away from him.

After Mike and Doc left, she and Eli had explored the mountainside, enjoying their time together even if their hunt for the missing rogues was unsuccessful. They'd returned to the cabin for a leisurely dinner, and then spent the night in each other's arms. The sex had been great even if a bit desperate at times. Both of them were painfully aware of their precious few hours together flying by, this private interlude drawing to an end.

That didn't mean she was going to waste a single second on regrets. She opened the oven to check the cookies. She set the tray on the stovetop to cool and turned off the oven. "I meant to tell you how much I liked your friends."

Eli looked up from the gun he was cleaning at the kitchen table. "They're good guys, both of them. You can trust them to do right by you."

Something in his voice made her think he wasn't talking in generalities. "Is there a reason you think I'll need to trust them?"

The lines of his cheekbones and jawline looked sharper than usual, as if recent events had worn away the last vestiges of softness in his face. "I hope not, but maybe."

He set the gun aside and joined her by the counter. "They think those men I told you about are still hunting for me. I'll deal with whatever they lob in my direction, but I won't risk you getting caught up in my mess. Mike wants me to check in with him or Doc at least every other day. If they don't hear from me, they'll come running. I asked them to make sure you're safe."

Before she could say a word, he put his fingers over her mouth. "And, yes, you have all those kickass moves and can defend yourself. But these guys aren't like anything you've ever encountered. They're black ops with deep pockets and powerful friends."

"They have no reason to come after me, and I hate that

they want you."

"Me, too."

She shivered in response to his grim acceptance of the situation and leaned into the warm strength of Eli's bare chest. He whispered near her ear, "Let it go for now. I've got other things on my agenda at the moment."

"Like what for instance?"

"Like picking up where we left off right before breakfast."

The heat in his smile sent a whole different kind of shiver through to her core. Neither of them had felt the need to get fully dressed when they'd finally rolled out of bed. He wore a pair of flannel pajama bottoms, while the soft cotton T-shirt she'd stolen from his closet was the only thing she had on. It meant for a lot of skin-to-skin contact and easy access for wandering hands to explore.

His fingertips traced an intricate pattern on her back before moving on to tug up the hem of her shirt. "So what do you think? Unless you have other plans for the morning, I suggest we adjourn to the other room."

Safara did a little exploring of her own, slipping her hands beneath the elastic waistband of his pajama bottoms. When she gave his ass a hard squeeze, his hips flexed forward, pressing his burgeoning erection against her belly. "I like the way you think."

One kiss led to another and another before they finally moved out of the kitchen. She was pretty sure he originally intended for them to end up back in bed, but they only made it as far as the couch. The space was cramped, not that she was complaining. It just led to more creativity on both their parts, along with a lot of giggling, a few curses, and potentially a bruise or two.

When they both finally collapsed in a boneless heap, Safara was limp but strangely energized at the same time. When Eli didn't seem inclined to move off of her, she tugged on his hair. "You need to move."

He didn't budge an inch as he muttered, "Why?"

"Because I need to breathe sometime today."

It took him several more seconds to make any effort to comply with her request. Finally, he pushed himself up to his elbows, giving her lungs the room they needed to work. He appeared fascinated by the movement of her chest. "Um, my eyes are up here, Eli."

"I know that." Not that he apparently cared.

When he finally rolled to the side, his main motivation seemed to be to use his free hand to capture one of her breasts. He began kneading it gently, smiling as his eyes drifted shut. If she didn't get moving, she'd be stuck there on the couch with him snoring softly in her ear. There were worse fates, but she did need to get moving.

With some determined wiggling and a few hard shoves, she managed to make her escape. After retrieving her T-shirt, she picked up Eli's pajama bottoms and tossed them on his head. "I'm going to take a shower."

He mumbled something in reply that she didn't quite catch. She launched one more salvo as she headed toward the bathroom. "You're welcome to join me. I promise to make it worth your while."

She must have scored a direct hit. Eli charged up off the couch and swept her into his arms before she made it halfway down the hall. Together, they cranked the shower up to steaming hot.

FOR THE SECOND time in two days, Eli's pleasant morning was interrupted by the sound of a vehicle approaching the cabin. Who could it be this time? Not Mike or Doc, for sure. They'd call first.

It seemed doubtful that the black-ops guys would come driving up in broad daylight, which didn't leave a whole lot of other possibilities. In fact, he could think of only one likely suspect. Praying he was wrong, he peeked out the front window. Yep, that was Jakes Dennell's cruiser. Damn. He hustled back to rap his knuckles on the bathroom door. "Safara, your father is pulling up out front."

She popped open the door, her eyes wide with panic. "Are you sure it's him?"

"It's his car. I didn't think you'd want to be running around the cabin naked right now. Not that I personally would mind, but I have a feeling he might have a different opinion on the subject."

Safara rolled her eyes. "You think? Stall him for as long as you can."

He laughed and got out of her way as she bolted for the bedroom to get dressed. "I'll try to entertain him for a few minutes, but somehow I don't think he'll be okay with that for long."

After fumbling with the buttons on his shirt on the way back to the living room, he stopped to pick up the couch cushions he'd knocked onto the floor in his haste to take Safara up on her invitation to share the shower. When he finally opened the door, Chief Dennell was already sporting a pretty unhappy expression. That was nothing compared to the one when he got a good look at Eli. His hand held a rolled-up newspaper, which he patted against the side of his leg. Eli suspected he'd rather be pounding him with it.

"I need to talk to my daughter." He gave Eli's chest a pointed look. "That is, if she's not too busy right now."

Confused, Eli glanced down at his shirt only to realize he'd buttoned the damn thing crooked. Well, shit, now what should he do? Her father hadn't been all that fond of Eli to begin with, and being confronted with some pretty damning evidence about how he and Safara had spent the morning clearly wasn't helping.

"Would you like to come in to wait? She should be along any second." If there was a God in heaven, anyway.

Jakes sighed, looking much older than he had the last time Eli had seen him. That prompted him to ask, "Is your father doing all right?"

"Yeah, other than he's getting more cantankerous by the minute. By the way, he'd like to thank you personally for helping him when you can spare a minute from . . ." He stopped midthought, probably realizing there was no good way to end that sentence. "Anyway, when you get a chance to stop by to see him, he'd appreciate it. Meanwhile, I could use a cup of coffee if you have one."

"Sure thing. Come on in."

Jakes headed straight for the kitchen. He tossed the newspaper onto the table and sat down.

Meanwhile, Eli plated up Safara's cookies and poured them each a cup of coffee. He was painfully aware of the muffled noises Safara made moving around in the next room. What the hell was taking her so long? Suddenly he was flashing back to the previous morning and their mad dash to hide any evidence they were more than just friends from Mike and Doc. When it came to Safara's father, that boat had sailed.

At this point, the silence between them had grown awkward. He reached for another cookie only to bump hands with Jakes, who was doing the same thing. It was hard not to laugh. They were both trying to avoid conversation by keeping their mouths full of cookie crumbs. Obviously the man wasn't happy to learn his Kalith daughter had spent the past two days holed up in a remote cabin with a human male.

Eli considered telling him that wasn't exactly the case. Well, the spending time with Eli was true enough, but he wasn't completely human. The trouble was that in Jakes's estimation, he might be exactly the worst possible kind of almost human he could be—a Paladin. He suspected pointing out that he and Safara knew they had no future together wouldn't make her father any happier. Fine. It didn't make Eli happy, either.

The extended silence had become unbearable. "More coffee?"

"I'm good."

Wow, they'd managed a whole four-word conversation without ripping into each other. Under the circumstances, that was a victory. To celebrate, he reached for another cookie.

The sound of the bedroom door opening had both men sitting up and staring toward the living room. By that point,

Eli didn't know which of them was more anxious for Safara to put in an appearance. He got up to pour her a cup of coffee, more to give himself something to do than looking as if he was about to pounce the second she came into sight.

At first glance, she appeared poised and not at all rattled by her father's unexpected appearance on Eli's doorstep. It was nice one of them could put up a good front.

She kissed Jakes on the cheek. "Hi, Dad. What brings you up here this morning?"

"You hadn't checked in recently. I'm your father and entitled to worry." He glanced in Eli's direction before adding, "We both know this mountain is a dangerous place right now."

Eli bit back the urge to laugh. They all knew the danger Jakes referred to had nothing to do with Safara's cousin and the other rogues who might be prowling the area. In fact, it was standing right there in the kitchen holding out a cup of coffee to his daughter.

Safara smiled her thanks and then sat down at the table. "So why didn't you just call? It would've saved you the long drive up here."

"I planned to take your place standing watch." After another one of his narrow-eyed glances at Eli, he added, "You've got better, more important things to do with your time."

Okay, he might've been talking about her job or spending time with her grandfather at the hospital, but that's not how Safara took it.

"If you're speaking as my boss, you have every right to reassign me to other duties. Say the word, and I'll head back home and go on patrol." Then she leaned in over the table, her pale eyes shooting sparks at Jakes. "But if as I suspect you're up here to play the overprotective father card, you can just drive back down the mountain and mind your own damn business."

That she spoke with a deadly calm didn't do anything to lessen the anger that hovered between the two Dennells. Eli didn't know whether to applaud her determination or slap his hand over her mouth before she said something that couldn't be erased. He had no intention of being the pry bar that tore apart the close relationship she had with her father.

It didn't help that Jakes wouldn't back down. "We've had this discussion, Safara. He's not our kind. He has no past that I can find. And it's pretty damn convenient that the only two people who could confirm his right to move into this cabin are both dead—Martin and his grandson. I even contacted Martin's attorney to find out what the hell is going on with this guy. He claimed attorney-client privilege and refused to answer any of my questions. The bottom line is that no one knows a damn thing about this guy or, if they do, they're afraid to talk."

She gasped in outrage, but she clamped her mouth shut, her lips edged in white at the effort it took to keep it that way. Safara knew the truth about Eli. But even at great cost to herself, she was clearly determined to protect his secrets.

He settled for putting his hand on her shoulder. "Safara, he's right. We talked about all the reasons why you can't get tangled up in my life."

"But—" She started to protest, but then stopped. "You're right. We did talk about it. We also talked about why you shouldn't get tangled up in mine. That doesn't seem to have stopped it from happening anyway."

Yeah, the entire situation sucked big-time, but it was what it was. The pain in her voice echoed his own feelings, but they both knew this fantasy world they'd been living in couldn't last forever. He wanted to punch someone, and the only handy target was off-limits. He might hate Jakes for dragging them both back into reality, but the man was only looking out for his own.

Jakes might be happy or at least relieved he'd gotten his way, but he had the good sense not to show it. If he'd acted even slightly smug, Eli might well have taken a swing at him and damn the consequences. He flexed his hand on Safara's shoulder, needing that small connection to maintain control.

Jakes abruptly broke off glaring at his daughter and Eli in turn and tapped the newspaper with his forefinger. "We've got more pressing problems right now."

It took Eli a few seconds to catch up with the change in subject. Safara reached for the paper and spread it out where the two of them could see the front page. The banner headline read "Unidentified Gang Goes on Bloody Rampage."

Safara looked stricken. "Oh no. What are we going to do?"

Eli skimmed the article, which outlined a series of apparently random attacks by a group armed with swords. The people involved wore odd clothing and had long hair. It was suggested that they looked like a group of reenactors of some kind or possibly a religious cult.

He dropped the paper back onto the table. "We're going to do whatever it takes to stop them."

Jakes pounded the table with his fist. "It's not your fight. It's ours."

Turning his attention back to his daughter, he continued, "I've already contacted the clan leaders. First up, we need to locate Tiel and the others. When we know where they've gone to ground, we'll organize the hunt."

Safara stood up. "It won't take me long to get my stuff together."

Eli wasn't about to get shoved to the sidelines now. It was time to make sure Jakes understood that. "They've already attacked your father and damn near killed him. They also attacked a Sworn Guardian and his men, not to mention Tiel did his best to kill your daughter. For that alone, he deserves to die."

He moved behind Safara and wrapped his arms around her shoulders and pulled her back against his chest. "I have years of the right kind of training for this kind of mission, all thanks to the U.S. Army and the Special Forces. Whether you approve of my involvement with your daughter or not, you're smart enough to use every asset at your disposal. Either include me in the plans, or I start hunting myself."

Then he offered the other man a predatory smile. "And I guarantee you, I have a helluva lot more experience in taking down rabid animals than you do. So, what's it going to be?"

The lawman glared at him. "You're not one of my deputies."

Safara tipped her head back against Eli's shoulder, clearly in no hurry to leave his embrace. "Neither are the clan leaders you're calling in to help. Eli's right, Dad. You can use his help, and you know it."

The two Dennells stared at each other for a long time before Jakes finally nodded.

"I'll go back to the office and track any new police reports. I'll feed you the information as I have it."

That gave Eli an idea. "Let's look at a map of the area and see where the attacks happened. That could give us a place to start."

He brought out the atlas he'd used to mark the locations of the previous attacks he'd researched at the library. When he opened to the map of Washington, Jakes leaned down to read the sticky notes, which had dates and locations written on them. "What are those?"

"More cases like the ones in today's paper. I did some checking when I was trying to figure out what happened to Martin. This kind of attack has been going on for years up and down the West Coast. I meant to tell Safara what I'd learned, but it slipped my mind with everything else that's been going on."

"Well, damn." Jakes ran his fingers through his salt-and-pepper hair as he stared down at the map and the story the small pieces of paper told. "Believe it or not, we do our best to control the incursions from Kalithia, but we can't catch every rogue that slips across."

Eli might have his differences with Jakes, but there was no way the man should have to shoulder a shitload of guilt for what the crazies from Kalithia had done over the years. Even with the best equipment, the best training, and even the best laid plans, sometimes things just went to hell for no good reason. When that happened, innocent people died. Eli had personal experience with that, and not just when that blasted helicopter crashed. Over the years, he'd learned the hard way that a man could either let failure cripple him or use it to reaffirm his resolve to do better the next time.

"No, you can't stop them, not completely. You know as well as I do that crazies are going to do what crazies do, whether we're talking about rogues from Kalithia or our own homegrown nutcases."

Then he met Jakes's gaze head-on, one warrior to another, and pointed at the newspaper headline again. "But we can stop this bunch and make sure they don't hurt anyone else."

He felt Safara tense as they waited for her father to respond. Finally, Jakes nodded. "You're right. Let's get these bastards."

16

Eli caught her arm before Safara could follow her dad outside. His deep green eyes crinkled at the corners, softening the grim expression on his face but not banishing it completely. "Tell him whatever you need to, Safara. Don't let my problems damage your relationship with your father. I'm not worth it."

And that kind of selfless act was what drew her heart like no other man she'd ever known regardless of their promises to keep their relationship simple. It was far too late for that. Rather than have that particular discussion right now, she gave Eli a quick kiss and followed her father out to his car. She could've waved good-bye from the porch, but there was too much left unsaid between them to let him just drive away. He started to open the door but stopped to lift his face up to the warm sunlight filtering through the trees. Maybe he'd also realized that they needed to talk things out.

With his eyes still trained on the sky, he muttered, "I should've called first."

"Yeah, you should have." She leaned her head against his

shoulder. "And I should've checked in again, so you wouldn't worry about me being up here alone."

Her dad's mouth curved up in the barest hint of a smile. "If you were alone, I wouldn't have been worried. Well, at least not about the same things."

She wanted to laugh, but knowing her time with Eli continued to tick down hurt too much. "No matter what happens or doesn't happen between Eli and me, he's a good man, Dad."

His smile disappeared as quickly as it had appeared. "I've learned to trust your people instincts. I just wish I knew more about him."

"Here's what I can tell you. You were right about Eli having secrets, ones he shared with me before the two of us . . . well, let's just say neither of us wanted our relationship to be based on lies. He knows my secrets, too."

She glanced back toward the man standing on the porch, his arms crossed over his chest, and smiled. He gave her a slow nod and then disappeared back into the cabin to afford her and her father more privacy.

"However, he told me I should share his with you, too, because he doesn't want to cause problems between us. I won't tell you everything, but I'll tell you this much—he's not Martin's distant relative. He's Martin's grandson, the one who died in that helicopter crash."

She paused to let that much sink in. It didn't take long for her father to connect the dots and come up with the right answer. "I'd heard rumors that Martin's father was Kalith, not that you would've guessed it from looking at him. Maybe my dad would know for sure since he and Martin were friends."

Her father turned around to lean against the fender of his car. "If Eli walked away from a fatal helicopter crash, then we both know which genes he inherited from Martin's side of the family. He's a Paladin, with all that means. Does he know?"

"He does now. I told you both Vedin and I assumed he was a Paladin. As it turns out, we were right about that."

"You know he'll develop a compulsion to be near the barrier now that he lives up here on the mountain, and it will only grow stronger over time. That could cause problems for our people who want to cross from one world into the other even if it isn't the light disease driving them to do it. They're not going to appreciate running into him, and it could turn violent quickly."

He wasn't telling her anything she didn't already know. She hadn't thought to tell Eli that, but she should have. Her father was talking again. "Our people tell a lot of stories about Paladins, most of them the stuff of nightmares."

"But he's not like that."

"I never said he was. Let me finish before you rip into me." When she nodded, he picked up where he'd left off. "Now, I figure our picture of what it means to be a Paladin is probably about as accurate as them thinking that all Kalith are crazed killers. Having said that, there are a few things about them that I do believe are true. One is that compulsion to be near the barrier."

Okay, she believed that. She'd seen Eli's reaction when she first introduced him to the barrier. Clearly awestruck by its awful beauty, he'd wanted to touch it. He'd also been reluctant to walk away from it, both on that occasion and later when she'd helped Vedin and his men return to their world.

Her father kept right on talking. "You already know they can heal from almost anything that doesn't involve dismemberment, and I've heard rumors that even that's possible if their medics get to them fast enough."

She hadn't asked Eli how he had died, and she never would. If he ever felt compelled to tell her, she'd listen, even if the picture of him injured and trapped in a burning helicopter had already given her nightmares.

Then she realized her father was frowning at her. "What?"

"Have you been listening to me at all?"

"Yes, you said Paladins need to be near the barrier and that their ability to heal is far stronger than what most Kalith have. Do you think that there's something about their human DNA that enhances that ability?"

He frowned as if giving the matter some thought. "I've never heard that was why, but it only makes sense that the mix of genes would produce some interesting results, some better than others."

She didn't like the sound of that last part. "Meaning?"

"All Paladins have an immense capacity for violence and a higher tolerance for its effects than other folks, both human and Kalith. Over the years, I've met a few people who have witnessed them in action. Everybody says the same thing—those bastards are hard-core killers, every last one of them."

He held up his hand to stave off her protest. "Honey, I do realize they're protecting their world, but it's also part of who they are. I'd go so far as to say that the ones like your Eli who don't know what they are often end up in the military or maybe law enforcement for a reason. If that inborn need to fight, to protect, isn't given the right focus, they might have problems dealing with how normal folks live."

Once again, she protested. "Eli is not like that."

She wasn't sure which one of them she was trying to convince, but she suspected she failed in either case. After all, she'd seen Eli charge into battle twice without hesitation, once against what should've been overwhelming odds. Not that she was complaining. After all, he'd been trying to save her ass on both occasions. But now that her father had brought up the subject, she had noticed that Eli had seemed remarkably unaffected by the incidents. Maybe that was his military training, but maybe not.

"Well, I'd better be going. As soon as I learn anything, I'll let you and Eli know." He gave her a quick hug. "Don't be in any rush to get back to town. The other deputies will cover your shifts for the next three days. They're glad to get the overtime, and the town can afford it. Besides, you never use as much vacation time as you're entitled to take."

"Thanks, Dad." She kissed his cheek. "One way or another, we'll take care of these rogues. This has been hard on all of us. I'll be glad when things settle down again."

"Me, too." As he opened the car door, his shoulders slumped. "I just have a hard time forgetting that each of those rogues is leaving behind someone who loves them."

Like her mother had.

There wasn't anything Safara could say that hadn't been said a hundred times before. Knowing the disease had already destroyed the woman her mother had once been didn't make the manner of her death any easier to accept.

"Tell Granddad to behave."

Her father's laugh sounded rusty. "Yeah, like that ever works with him."

He gave the cabin one last pointed look. "Tell Eli that his secret is safe with me as long as it doesn't cause problems for me or the people of my town."

"I will."

Not that she liked the way he qualified his promise, but there wasn't much she could do about it. She watched him drive away, waving one last time. When his car disappeared around the bend, she headed right back into the waiting arms of the man who had stepped out onto the porch.

"HOW DID HE take the news?"

Although Eli could guess, having watched the last few minutes of their conversation from his front window. Their body language had conveyed a mix of emotions, some of them pretty volatile. At least by the time Jakes drove away, he and Safara had come to some kind of truce. That was good. He'd meant what he'd said about not wanting to cause a rift between Safara and her family.

She shrugged. "Better than expected. The good news is that he put me in for vacation for the next three days, so I don't have to rush back to work."

That was good news. Sort of, anyway. With what Mike had told him, Eli figured he'd have to disappear soon and establish a new identity somewhere else, most likely in another country. He wouldn't risk the danger from the men who were hunting him spilling over onto his friends.

Unfortunately, the more time he and Safara spent together, the harder it was going to be to leave her behind. It would already hurt like hell. But before they could think about that, they had some killers to track down.

"I looked up more information online about the attacks. There have been a few more sightings, including at a small grocery store that was robbed right before dawn. There were no security cameras, but witnesses gave descriptions that fit the rogues. I've plotted all the data. I want you to look at the map, because I think I'm seeing a pattern. If so, it could be a good starting point."

Once inside, he stood back while Safara studied the map. She leaned in closer to read the times and brief descriptions he'd written on the sticky notes. Finally, she nodded as she pointed to a couple of icons on the map that indicated a campground.

"You're thinking they hole up in this state park and go on raids from there."

Good, she saw it, too. "There haven't been any incidents reported at that site so far, but all the known locations of sightings and attacks are within easy walking distance of the park. It would make sense they'd take shelter somewhere they'd have access to water and bathrooms."

Safara looked grim. "As much as they crave the light in this world, it takes time to acclimate to it. Since the store is right outside of the park, I'm betting that was their last stop before they went to ground for the day. I'll call Dad."

Yeah, she should do that, but he wasn't going to sit on the sidelines and wait for Jakes to round up his crew. The rogues might've taken shelter for the daylight hours, but eventually they'd be out prowling again. When that happened, more people would get hurt or killed.

"Give him a heads-up and tell him we'll update him after we scout around. No use in him sending everyone on a wild-goose chase if we're wrong about this."

Safara hesitated, but then she finally nodded. "He won't like it, but there's not much he can do to stop us."

Eli grabbed the broadsword down off the wall and slid it into its sheath. He laid it on the kitchen table next to Safara's own blade. He'd been meaning to ask her about it. "I take it that style is the weapon of choice in Kalithia."

"Yes. They're handed down from one generation to the next. It's one of my most prized possessions."

She traced the intricate engraving on the blade of her sword and then glanced at Martin's weapon collection. "It's a beautiful work of art, and the Kalith who made it was as much of an artist as he was a bladesmith. I wish I never had to do anything but admire it hanging on my wall."

What could he say to that? As a Special Forces soldier, his use of weapons had become second nature to him. He'd served his country and had been proud to do so. It was hard to put into words why it was important that someone had to be willing to carry a gun or even a sword and stand ready to use it. For Safara's sake, he'd try.

"There are always going to be people in this world who are a clear and present danger to those around them. Someone has to stand against that kind of evil."

When Safara winced, he eased closer to her and weighed his next words carefully. "Your mother was not evil. This sickness drove her to do what she did. It's doing the same with these rogues. That doesn't change the fact that someone has to put a stop to their violence. Not everyone is strong enough to take on that job, and those of us who do pay a high price for it."

She turned into his embrace, resting her head against his chest. It felt so right holding her close and drawing comfort from each other. After a few seconds, she whispered, "And if I'm not strong enough? You know, to defend both worlds?"

Safara was as strong as anyone he'd ever served with, but he also understood what she was feeling right now. "Sweetheart, we all have moments of doubt. When that happens, we draw strength from those who stand beside us in the battle. Barring that, we dig down deep and find it in ourselves. It's what makes us who we are."

He shared his biggest shame. "I left my friends dead on that mountainside. I picked myself up, dusted myself off, and just walked away. I panicked over watching my body stitch itself back together. I couldn't stay and face the consequences of surviving."

She pushed back far enough to look up at him. "Anyone who didn't know such things were possible would've reacted that way."

"I can't speak for anyone else, but it felt pretty damn cowardly to walk away. I don't know what possibility I feared more—that they'd eventually believe me or that they wouldn't. How could I face the family and friends of the men who died that day? Their loved ones died, and I walked away without an effing scratch to show for it."

Right now she was still trying to defend his actions. "Eli, even if you didn't know it at the time, your decision to leave that mountain protected the secrets of the Paladins and my people. If you think people would've freaked out because you survived, how do you think they'd react to finding out that aliens exist and have been living among humans for who knows how long?"

All right, that was quite a stretch, enough that he could only laugh. "So I get credit for an accidental benefit from hauling ass away from a crazy situation? I'm not sure the army would look at it that way. In fact, I suspect they'd be pretty upset to find out that I haven't told them about a possible threat to the country's security."

"What makes you think they don't already know about us? Or maybe the Paladins? Those black-ops guys must have some reason to be hunting for you."

"That thought had crossed my mind, but there's no way to know for sure." He gave her another quick hug while he still had the chance. "But we need to move out soon. I want to scout out that park. Once we've assessed the situation, we'll contact your dad and decide on a plan of attack."

He hesitated before finally saying, "I can do the recon by myself if you want to stay here or even go help your dad rally the troops."

"I'm not letting you walk into a fight by yourself." Safara picked up her sword. "I have to do this, Eli. Lives depend on it."

Next, she tapped the badge pinned to her shirt. "I swore an oath to serve and protect. I mean to keep that promise."

His heart did a slow roll in his chest. Damn, she was magnificent. A man could face anything life threw at him with a woman like her at his side. Too bad it wouldn't be him.

But the image of her with another man, sharing what the two of them had shared during the night, had him clenching his fists. Too bad the lucky bastard, whoever he might be, wasn't standing right there in front of him. The two of them would have a heartfelt—and possibly hands-on—conversation about Safara and how she deserved to be treated.

"Eli, are you okay? I don't know where you went in your head just now, but it can't be a happy place."

No, it damn well wasn't. He wasn't about to explain that he was imagining how good it would feel to beat the crap out of some guy he'd never met. Eli had no right to stake a claim on Safara when he had no future to offer her. Right now, though, he wasn't thinking about right and wrong. They had places to go, bad guys to round up, but he wasn't thinking about that, either.

There was only one thing he wanted—needed. And that was Safara. Anywhere he could have her, any way he could have her.

Smart woman that she was, she backed away. "Eli? What's going on?"

He followed her step for step. "Nothing is going on. In fact, a few things are about to come off."

To show her what he had in mind, he peeled off his shirt and then reached for the button on his jeans. She swallowed hard and took another step back. Didn't she know never to show weakness in front of a predator? And God knows he was feeling pretty damn predatory at the moment. If she'd shown any real fear, he would've backed off instantly. But she wasn't looking scared, not with the way she just licked her lips and dragged her gaze down his body to stare at the front of his jeans. He tugged the zipper down an inch. When her eyes flared wide and hot, he tugged it down a little more.

He glanced at the sword clutched in her hand. "You'd better set that down unless you plan to use it on me."

"We don't have time for this, Eli."

Despite her protest, she carefully laid the sword on the table. He prowled another two steps in her direction. "We should make time."

She started to back away again, but then her chin came up in challenge as she stood her ground. "What's really going on here?"

"I already answered that question. I think it's your turn to take something off. Anything at all would be fine, but I'm thinking your jeans would be a step in the right direction." He grinned at her, letting her see the hunger raging through him. "I'd be glad to help with that, and I promise to make it worth your while."

"I don't know what's gotten into you."

Truth was, he didn't, either. However, he did know exactly what he wanted to get into her. She was right about one thing, though. They really didn't have time for a long, drawn-out seduction. It was time to end the discussion and get with the program.

Using those fancy Paladin reflexes she'd told him about, he lunged close enough to grab her by the waist and pressed her against the nearest wall. As he captured her mouth with his, he reached for the snap on her jeans. After popping it open, he slid the zipper down. With his fingers teasing at the waistband of her panties, he rested his forehead against hers. "Tell me you want this, too."

She stared into his eyes for a few heartbeats before nodding. "Yes."

Her sad smile made it clear that he wasn't the only one who knew their time together was nearly over, and the world outside was going to demand its due from them both. That's all it took. He kissed her luscious mouth, loving that she gave as good as she got. He worked his hand down inside her panties to palm her core and gently squeezed.

She gasped and rocked her hips hard against the pressure. He broke off the kiss and stooped to peel her jeans and panties down to her ankles, where the process came to a screeching halt thanks to her boots. He dropped down to one knee to untie them. It took him two attempts to get the job done thanks to shaky hands and the temptation to stay right where he was and pleasure his woman a different way.

Instead, he carried her across the room and tumbled them both onto the couch in a tangle of arms and legs. By now she was just as eager to finish what he'd started. He shoved his jeans out of the way and got down to business. This was no gentle wooing, there was no finesse, just the overwhelming urge to make Safara his again, even if only for these last few minutes. They came together again and again, the urgency building with each stroke and each touch.

She chanted his name between demands for more. He willingly gave her everything he had, including his heart. When the tempest between them reached its crescendo, he was pretty sure he died for the second time. Maybe he just wished he had, because if this was his last time with Safara, he wasn't sure he wanted to go on living.

But unfortunately, life went on. They both had rogues

to hunt and two worlds to protect. He kissed her one more time. It was soft and sweet and tasted so damn sad.

17

They were almost back to the highway when Eli's phone rang. He stopped long enough to fish it out of his pocket. He muttered a curse after seeing the number and swiped his finger across the screen.

"What's wrong?"

Why would he assume there was a problem? She waited while he listened for several seconds before saying another word. When he did, it was both colorful and obscene. "Fine. I'm parked at the bottom of the road that leads up to my cabin. Safara and I will wait here for you."

Eli shoved the phone back into his pocket. At first he didn't seem inclined to explain what was going on, but finally he turned the engine off and slouched back in his seat. "That was Doc. He and Mike are about five minutes out."

Then he banged his fist against the steering wheel hard enough that she half expected it to break. "Why does everything have to go all to hell at the same time?"

He didn't stick around long enough for her to respond, instead slamming out of the truck to pace up and down the road. She gave him a few seconds to work off a bit of his temper before venturing out herself.

"What's happened?"

He shook his head and kept moving. Eventually he would run out of steam or his friends would arrive and confirm what she already suspected: The problem with the men hunting Eli had escalated. Not what either of them needed right now, but then life rarely scheduled a crisis for a convenient time.

It wasn't long before the sound of a vehicle approaching brought Eli's pacing to an abrupt halt. "Get behind the truck and keep your head down."

The man was good at giving orders but piss poor at giving explanations. Now wasn't the time for arguments, so she did what he told her. That didn't mean they wouldn't revisit the situation in the future. Meanwhile, a large SUV appeared from around the corner. Its heavily tinted windows made it impossible to make out more than the vague shapes of the two men inside. Eli remained on full alert until the driver's window rolled down and Doc stuck his head out.

"Are you going to shoot at us? Because I'm telling you right now, I'm not in the mood."

Eli lowered his gun but kept scanning the area rather than focusing on his friends. "I thought we were all going to lie low and only get in touch in an emergency."

Doc looked thoroughly disgusted. "We did, and it is. An emergency, that is."

The passenger door on the SUV opened and Mike stepped out. He was sporting bruises on his face and had his left arm in a sling.

Safara left her hiding spot next to the truck and hurried

over to join the three men. "What happened?"

"Someone tried to run me off the road by shooting my tire." Mike winced and shifted his stance as if looking for a position that didn't hurt quite so much. "When that didn't work, they nudged my car over into the ditch. Since they didn't stick around to finish the job, they didn't necessarily want to kill me, although they probably wouldn't have lost any sleep if they had. More likely it was a warning to quit poking my nose where it doesn't belong."

Since Eli didn't show any signs of asking for clarification, she did it for him. "And that's what you've been doing?"

Mike flexed the fingers on his injured arm. "Evidently."

Eli picked up a handful of rocks and heaved them at the nearest tree hard enough to send chips of bark flying. "Damn it, Mike, I told you to walk away. Let them come after me directly."

By this point, Mike's easygoing stance had morphed into his pissed-off commanding officer mode. "Sergeant, do not presume to give me orders. You may not be on active duty, but you are still one of my men. If someone is hunting you, they have to go through me first."

Doc started to step between his two friends, but Eli shoved him out of the way to glare down at Mike. "You could've been killed. I can't have that on my conscience. Not now, not ever."

Mike glared right back. "It's my choice. Any consequences, good or bad, are on me, not you."

As a deputy, Safara sometimes used her gender to ratchet down the tension when the situation called for it. With that in mind, she shoved her way between the two men. Just as she'd expected, each of them immediately took an immediate half step backward to give her room.

"That's enough, both of you." She put her hands on her hips and stared at each of them in turn. "I think we can agree on the fact that each of you cares deeply what happens to the other. It's also obvious you should be combining forces against your common enemy, not threatening each other."

While she waited for them to come to their senses, she glanced at Doc to see how he was reacting to her butting into the situation. To her surprise, he grinned and winked at her. Nice to know he approved.

Surprisingly, Eli was the first to back down. "Look, you and Doc go on up to the cabin. Safara and I have some unfinished business to deal with, and I'm not sure how long it will take. When I get back, we can make plans about what to do next. Until then, help yourself to anything you need."

He maintained eye contact with Mike when he added, "I'm thinking it's time that I move on. I've already decided to leave the country and disappear completely. That way, these guys won't have any more reasons to come after you."

Wait. When had Eli made that decision? It better have been just this second. Safara was going to turn violent if he'd known all along he was going to leave this soon and hadn't bothered to tell her. Yes, they'd agreed any long-term involvement wasn't in the cards for the two of them, but she hadn't realized that he planned to cut off all future contact not only with her, but with his friends as well. The pain cut right through her heart, leaving her bleeding and hurt on the inside, not that she'd let it show on the outside. Like the man said, they had other business to finish. Then she'd walk away, head held high, and pick up the pieces of her life.

"We'd better go, Eli, while we still have enough hours of daylight left."

He nodded without looking in her direction. She fought a childish urge to hop up and down waving her hands in his face to force him to acknowledge she was standing right there in front of him.

"What the fuck? Eli, are those swords hanging in the rifle rack in the back window of your truck?"

Without waiting for an answer, Doc opened the passenger door of Eli's pickup and reached inside. Safara groaned when he pulled out her sword and held it up for everyone to see as if he expected her and Eli to be as surprised by its presence as he was.

"Put it back, Doc, before you hurt yourself. That blade is sharp."

As he spoke, Eli closed his eyes and rubbed his forehead like he had a headache coming on. She knew just how he felt. Mike headed over to look at the swords for himself while Eli remained rooted in place with a look of confused frustration on his face.

Doc went back to snooping. "You've also got enough firepower in here to outfit a battalion. Just what kind of unfinished business do you and Safara have going on today?"

Well, someone had to say something. When she couldn't come up with a logical reason that the two of them were so heavily armed, she went for simple. "I don't suppose you'd be willing to forget you ever saw any of that."

Doc looked at her as if she'd just sprouted a second head, while Mike snorted and shook his head. "Sorry, not happening."

By that point, they were both laughing. As irritating as it was, she couldn't really blame them. Nodding in their direction, she gave Eli a hard look. "They're your friends, so you explain. They'll come closer to believing you."

For the first time since Doc's phone call, Eli smiled, sort of. "Here's the thing, guys: We're on our way to scout out a state park looking for a bunch of sword-wielding crazies. We thought it only reasonable that we bring our own blades to the party."

There was nothing about his expression or the tone of his voice that said he was serious, but evidently Mike knew him well enough to see below the surface. "And how many crazies does it take to make a bunch?"

Eli's smile faded, and he looked to her for guidance. She took a deep breath and jumped off the cliff. "Tell them whatever you want. We both know they can keep a secret."

"There were eight at last count. The number may have gone up or down since then. We promised Safara's father, who is the chief of police for Ridgewick, that we'd take a casual look around the park. If he drove through in his cruiser, that might put innocent civilians in danger. If we spot them, he'll bring in the authorities."

Okay, neither man bought that story at all. Mike came back around the truck to confront Eli. "I know Safara here is a deputy, but the cops wouldn't send a civilian like you're pretending to be into a dangerous situation even armed to the teeth with guns, much less a sword. If they didn't want to alarm these alleged crazies, they'd send in one of their own undercover. All of that tells me her father doesn't want to go through normal channels to deal with the threat these people present."

Doc was busy looking up something on his phone. "Major, there are multiple reports in the area of folks being attacked by people carrying swords. The descriptions vary in some respects, but everyone agrees the perps speak heavily accented English, making it likely they're not originally from around here."

Eli had moved closer to where Safara stood, maybe to present a united front to his friends. At Doc's last comment, he leaned down to whisper, "That last bit is putting it mildly."

Mirroring their stance, Doc and Mike planted themselves right in front of her and Eli. "Now, Sergeant, what's really happening? No bullshit this time. That's an order, in case you've forgotten what they sound like."

"If I do tell you, Major, you have to swear to keep it a secret, no matter what."

Mike's chin came up in stubborn refusal. "No can do. I don't make promises without knowing the facts first."

Eli gave her a disgusted look when she snickered. "You're not helping matters, lady."

"Sorry, but as I recall, you said something similar to me when I asked you to keep your mouth shut when you wanted me to clue you in on this same subject."

She was right, and he knew it. "Fine, but understand there are innocent people at risk if this gets out."

Normally the more easygoing man, Doc looked serious as death. "What innocent people?"

It was time for her take control of the situation. The rogues were her problem, and the innocents Eli mentioned her responsibility. "Both the rogues and the innocents originate from Kalithia. I guess you could describe them as undocumented immigrants."

Mike exchanged a questioning look with Doc before saying, "I've served all over the world, and I've never heard of that place."

This time it was Eli who snickered. "There's a good reason for that."

When he didn't continue, the major's next words were heavily laced with temper. "Which would be?"

Eli held up his hand as if taking an oath. "I swear I'm not crazy, but Kalithia is another world, not another country. Evidently, I inherited my weird-ass ability to heal from some Kalithia-born ancestor."

"Bullshit!" Doc looked thoroughly disgusted. "If there are aliens in this world, why haven't I ever met one?"

"You have." Safara started to hold out her hand to reintroduce herself to Doc as his first official alien. Instead, she gave him a quick hug and pecked him on the cheek. "And now you've been kissed by one."

His face flushed red, whether from embarrassment or from temper it was hard to tell. He rubbed his cheek and stared at her for the longest time. Finally, he said, "Well, if you're an alien, at least you're better looking than E.T."

"Thanks—I think."

All four of them cracked up, laughing long and hard even if it had Mike wincing in pain. Maybe there was a bit of hysteria in their response, but at least they burned off some of the tension they'd all been feeling.

When the moment wound down, Doc rubbed his hands

together. "Okay, I don't know about the major here, but I'm all for kicking some alien butt. What's the plan?"

Her father wasn't going to be happy that she'd dragged two more outsiders into their business. But honestly, all things considered, she didn't know how else she could've handled the situation. Eli was looking to her for direction.

Once again, she pointed out the obvious. "They're your friends. You figure it out."

ELI CONSIDERED THE options and tried to figure out a way to keep his friends out of the line of fire. What he really wanted to do was toss Safara into their SUV and give them the job of keeping her under wraps until he and her father had dealt with the rogues. She would gut him with that sword of hers for even thinking such a thing, much less if he actually said it out loud. Before surrendering to the inevitable, he tried one last time to keep Mike and Doc safely on the sidelines.

"Like I said, this is a scouting expedition, but we all know even the best designed plans can blow up in your face in a heartbeat." He paused to point at Mike's arm. "You're in no shape for a fight."

The man wasn't buying it. "It's my left arm. I'm right-handed and can still pull a trigger."

If bullets started flying, they'd need every weapon they could get. "Fine, you can come, but you're providing support, not leading the charge. Agreed?"

He waited until Mike nodded before continuing. "I have an extra handgun one of you can use."

Doc answered for both of them. "We're good. When the

major called me to come get him, I thought it only wise to come loaded for bear."

"Okay, then. I think we should all ride together in your SUV rather than in a two-vehicle convoy. We'll draw less attention that way. Any questions?"

"What kind of firepower will the enemy have?"

Safara winced at Mike's description of her people, but she didn't protest. "In some ways, Kalithia is less mechanized than this world, so no guns. That doesn't mean they aren't dangerous. They fight with the traditional swords of our people, like mine over there in the truck."

She looked so damned sad as she continued her explanation. "Kalithia's sun is dying, and some of our people are susceptible to what we call the light disease. It drives its victims to seek the bright sun in this world. The illness slowly destroys their minds, leaving them out of their heads with the need to kill anyone who crosses their path. If they get close enough to attack, don't hesitate to pull the trigger. The person they used to be is already dead, and the truth is that you would be showing them mercy."

Eli added his own take on the situation. "We faced off against this bunch when eight of them attacked Safara at once. I'd like to say that I rushed in and singlehandedly saved the day, but that's not what happened. Four cops from Kalithia joined the fight on our side to help drive the rogues off. These people might be crazy, but they're damn good fighters."

By that point, both Doc and Mike had their game faces on. So did Safara, for that matter. Good. This was serious business, the kind he'd been dealing with since his first deployment. He'd missed working with a team of warriors all dedicated to making the world a better place. While this group might number fewer than the ones he'd deployed with in the past, there was no one he'd rather have at his side when facing potential danger.

"Let's transfer our gear to the SUV and then move out."

It was tempting to punch Doc when he offered Eli a sloppy salute and said, "Yes, sir. Happy to, sir. I live to serve."

"Remind me, Doc, why I used to like having you around."

Doc was already pulling stuff out of Eli's truck. "My charm, intelligence, and good looks?"

Both Eli and Mike shook their heads. "No, that's not it."

Eli dumped a lot more of the gear on top of the few things Doc had taken out of the truck. "Now I remember what it was that I liked about you."

His friend's eyes narrowed in suspicion. "And that would be?"

Eli clapped him on the shoulder. "You make a damn good pack mule."

Doc rolled his eyes as he lugged the heavy load over to his vehicle. "Very funny."

But to give the man credit, he grinned right along with the rest of them. Two minutes later, they pulled out onto the highway. The hunt was on.

18

By rights, as the only cop in the car, Safara figured she should be the one in the driver's seat, not sitting in the back while Doc ripped down the two-lane highway toward the park. She considered pointing that out to her companions, but there was no use starting a battle she wouldn't win. Not with this much testosterone packed into such a confined space.

"The entrance is about a mile farther up on the right."

Doc met her gaze in the rearview mirror with a smile. "Thanks."

When he frowned and quickly checked both outside mirrors, Eli joined the conversation. "What's wrong, Doc?"

"Probably nothing, but a dark blue pickup passed us going the other direction a couple of minutes ago. Now there's one right behind us. It might be a coincidence, but maybe not. Don't everybody start twisting around to get a look at him. He's close enough to notice."

They reached the entrance to the park and turned in. The truck whizzed past, continuing westbound on the highway, but it was too soon to breathe a sigh of relief. If the driver thought they'd noticed him, he might be trying to throw them off his scent.

Doc slowed to a stop. "What do you want me to do?"

It was time she took charge. "There's nothing we can do about him right now. Let's see if the rogues are here in the park."

Mike twisted around to face her. "So what are we looking for exactly? What will these people look like?"

She pointed at her eyes. "They'll have eyes roughly the color of mine. Their hair will be dark and shot through with silver, even the younger ones. And before you ask, I dye mine to hide the gray."

Something she hated doing, but she and her father both thought it was necessary. With so many Kalith living in and around Ridgewick, someone would be bound to notice a lot of young people all having salt-and-pepper hair even in their teens.

"The last time we saw them, they were dressed in dark tunics over trousers. That may have changed by now, but for sure they'll be carrying swords like mine."

She knew her duty and would see it carried out. Regardless, revealing her own people's existence to these men felt like a betrayal of everything she stood for. The knowledge that she might also have to execute the rogues made her sick at heart. Even if they did return home, it would be to face probable execution at the hands of the Sworn Guardians and their Blademates. There was no happy ending in sight for any of them.

Eli squeezed her hand. The small gesture meant a lot

even if she was still mad at him for announcing his decision to leave the country without talking to her about it first. Yet another item on their agenda that would have to be dealt with eventually.

But one thing at a time.

Doc started driving again, going slowly to give them all time to study their surroundings for any sign of the enemy. When Safara rolled her window down in order to hear better, the three men immediately followed suit. They were just turning down the last loop off the main road when a scream rang out. Doc hit the brakes as they all strained to determine which direction it had come from.

Mike leaned his head out of his window. "Anybody see anything?"

Eli did the same. "No."

Safara spotted movement in the woods off to the left. "There. Someone just ducked into those trees. I barely caught a glimpse of him, so I can't tell for sure. I'll go see. The rest of you keep hunting."

Eli was out the door and heading around to her side of the vehicle before she even had her seat belt unfastened. She looked at Mike. "Okay, let me rephrase that. Eli and I will check him out while you and Doc drive on ahead. We'll text you if we spot anything, and you do the same."

"Got it."

She and Eli started off across the clearing at a slow trot. They'd only gotten halfway when they heard terrified voices in counterpoint to dark laughter and taunts. They slowed to listen to triangulate the source of the sounds. Finally, Eli pointed into the distance. "There."

She drew both her service revolver and her sword. They kept moving forward, but more slowly while Eli called in their backup. Once they knew Mike and Doc were on their way, they picked up speed. By then they could clearly see two of the rogues and make out at least some of what was being said, none of it good. Tiel had cornered two adults, who had three young children huddled behind them.

The woman was pleading with him, her voice thick with tears and fear. "Please, mister, let my children go. They didn't do anything to you."

The Kalith jabbed the tip of his sword at the husband, slicing the man's arm open. From a distance, it was hard to tell how badly he was hurt as blood dripped down his arm.

Tiel kept waving his sword around in front of the couple. "Who wants to bleed next?"

Eli bellowed in fury. "Tiel, you worthless coward, I ran you off once, and I'll do it again."

His efforts to draw the rogue's attention away from the innocent campers worked, but only in part. Tiel charged right for them, but his companion remained to keep the humans from escaping. Eli lowered his weapon. "I don't have a clear shot."

He shoved his gun back into its holster and drew his broadsword. "I'll deal with your cousin. You see what you can do about the other guy."

She wished they could shoot the rogue, but the bastard was now using the children as human shields. At that point, Tiel and Eli came together with a clash of swords. To make matters worse, six more rogues were now headed right toward them. Several were sporting bandages, marking them as the same bunch they'd faced outside the cave. Good. It was time to end their rampage.

Where were Mike and Doc? Not that either of them would be of much use once she and Eli were surrounded by the enemy. Even if they had swords, they wouldn't know how to use them, and they couldn't risk using their guns for fear of hitting one of their own.

The sound of squealing tires was followed by several car doors opening, too many for it to be Mike and Doc. When she risked a glance back toward the road, her heart skipped a beat and then started beating far too fast when a tall man dressed all in black jumped out of the driver's door of the blue pickup truck that had been following them earlier. He calmly held up what looked like a sniper rifle and took aim. It was impossible to tell exactly who he had in his sights. She prayed it was one of the rogues.

At the same time, a group of four men had just piled out of a large van. Before the other man could pull the trigger, they had him surrounded. After they subdued their prisoner and tossed him into the bed of his truck, they drew swords and headed straight toward her and Eli at a dead run. Dear God, they were Paladins! Well, at least two of them were. The others carried Kalith swords even though they were dressed in human clothing.

She called out to Eli, "We've got company. Not sure if they're actually on our side, but they're definitely not on Tiel's."

The other rogues were nearly upon them. She prayed the humans would survive long enough for them or the Paladins to rescue them. Then a single shot rang out. The rogue behind the children dropped to the ground as Mike and Doc stepped into sight and herded the family back out of danger.

Good. None of them needed to see the bloodbath that was coming.

The rogues spread out to surround her and Eli. Two challenged her directly, one male and the other female. She had no choice but to take them both on, too busy trying to avoid being cut to pieces to keep track of the four newcomers.

A second later, a deep voice called out to her. "Officer, I'm coming up on your left. I'll take the male."

Under the circumstances, she wasn't going to argue. A dark-haired man moved up beside her. Now that he was so close, it was easy to see that he was Kalith. When he spotted her sword, he gave her a solemn nod and then went to work drawing the attention of her male opponent, leaving her free to deal with the female.

The fighting was vicious. Eli and the other men taunted their opponents, but she saved her breath. The Kalith woman had been a well-trained fighter at some point in the past, but in her disease-driven rage, she was taking reckless chances. That didn't make her any less dangerous. With little regard for her own survival, the woman attacked Safara with deadly intent. Clearly there would be no quarter given on either side.

The battle between the two Kalith males next to her was over in a matter of seconds, leaving the rogue bleeding out on the ground. His death cry briefly distracted her own opponent. The woman screamed in fury and turned her attack against the warrior who had come to Safara's aid. She'd always wondered if she had it in her to kill. As much as the idea sickened her, she found the strength to end the woman's existence. There would be an emotional price to be paid for that, but not right now.

The closest Paladin shouted at the remaining rogues, "Stand down, you sick sons of bitches, and we'll let you go home."

No one took him up on the offer, and the battle intensified until Tiel and Eli were the only two still fighting. Sweat poured off Eli's face as he tried to break through her cousin's defenses. Tiel had to know that if he succeeded in bringing down Eli, the grim-faced men who surrounded him would make damn sure he wouldn't escape.

The two Kalith warriors stood on either side of her as they watched the deadly battle continue. She hated to watch; at the same time, she couldn't look away. The only sounds were the loud clang of sword against sword and the heavy breathing of men quickly running out of breath and strength. In a quick move, Tiel raised his sword and prepared to swing it down in an arc intended to separate Eli's head from his shoulders.

She bit back the need to scream, not wanting to distract Eli. When he deflected the blow and shoved his blade straight into Tiel's chest, her cousin's fury quickly faded into confusion as he staggered back and slowly collapsed. Safara started forward, not sure which man needed her more at that moment. She chose the one she loved.

"Eli, are you all right?"

He had dropped his sword and stood bent over with his hands on his knees gasping for air. When he nodded and straightened up, she checked him over for damage. Other

ALEXIS MORGAN

than a few nicks and cuts, he'd survived the fight pretty much intact. His arms surrounded her, offering them the comfort they both needed.

"Safara?"

Tiel's voice was barely a whisper, but to her it sounded as if he'd shouted her name. Eli immediately released his tight hold on her but stayed nearby as she knelt at her dying cousin's side. She gently brushed Tiel's hair back from his face, taking his hand in hers. Using her other hand, she tried to staunch the blood gushing from his chest. It was a vain effort, and they both knew it.

His skin had taken on a bluish tinge, and his pale eyes were dull with pain as he struggled to talk. "Sorry... Couldn't stop."

She shushed him as her eyes blurred with tears. "I know, Tiel. Don't waste your strength."

"See that... my family knows..."

Those were the last words he spoke, but she answered anyway. "I will. I promise."

She remained kneeling as she prayed for the souls of all the dead and for their families and friends. All Kalith knew the pain of losing someone to the light disease, but it never got easier to deal with the despair and futility of it all.

Finally, Eli lifted her to her feet. She straightened her shoulders and braced herself to face the age-old enemies of her people and their Kalith allies.

19

This was far from the first time Eli had stood on a field of battle surrounded by the dead. It never got any easier. He hated to end Tiel's life, but the bastard had left him no choice. Or more correctly, the light disease had brought them both to this moment. At least it hadn't been Safara who'd dealt her cousin's death blow. That didn't change the fact the man had died along with the rest of the rogues.

And typical of such conflicts, there wasn't time to stand around and contemplate the nature of war. He had to find Mike and Doc to see how the civilians they'd herded away from the fighting were faring. Before that, he needed to deal with the four men who'd appeared out of nowhere to join the battle.

He noticed one of them had found plastic tarps somewhere to cover the dead. At least they treated the fallen with respect. For Safara's sake, he appreciated their thoughtfulness.

One of the four headed toward Eli and Safara. He was as tall as Eli, and his dark eyes reflected a wealth of experience with this kind of situation. While not openly hostile, neither was he exactly friendly. The fact they'd fought against a common enemy didn't necessarily translate into them being allies. Having said that, the four men had much in common with those he'd served with for years—a whole lot of attitude and the skills to back it up.

The stranger spoke first. "I'm Lonzo Jones."

He pointed toward the three men now moving up beside him. "This is Barak q'Young, Larem q'Jones, and Hunter Fitzsimon."

"I'm Eli Jervain, and this is Deputy Safara Dennell."

He'd let Mike and Doc introduce themselves later. Next, he pointed toward the pickup truck. "Is that guy a friend of yours?"

Lonzo glanced at his three companions and then shook his head. "We've never seen him before. Since we couldn't tell who he was about to shoot, we took him out of the equation."

"Good thinking."

Eli didn't tell them that if it turned out the guy was part of the bunch who'd run Mike off the road, he'd be joining the rogues under one of those blue tarps.

"Eli?"

Safara looked more pale than usual and worried as hell. Whether it was because of him, her cousin dying, or the fact she was standing there facing two men guaranteed to play into her worst fears was impossible to know. He did his best to shake off his dark thoughts for her sake. Time to get back on point. "So, care to tell me how you and your friends happened along at exactly the right time?"

Lonzo looked thoroughly disgusted. "I'd like to say it was our superior skills and general sneakiness, but it was mostly just dumb luck. We've been searching the area for those Kalith, and this just happened to be our next stop."

He then turned in Safara's direction. "Deputy Dennell, as you've probably guessed, my friends and I are part of the Seattle contingent of Paladins. I wish we were meeting under better circumstances. For what it's worth, we've been planning on reaching out to you and your father for some time now."

Her eyes opened wide in shock. "You have? Why?"

Lonzo gestured toward the other Paladin and one of the Kalith men. "Hunter here has been working with Larem to track down the Kalith who have crossed the barrier to live peacefully in this world."

She gasped and started to back away. Eli blocked her retreat. "Where are you going?"

He hated the very real fear in her eyes when she tried to sidestep him. "I've got to warn Dad and the others. They need time to get away."

Then she looked past Eli toward Lonzo and his companions. "My people are no danger to you or the humans in the area."

Lonzo was doing his best to look nonthreatening but couldn't quite pull it off, especially with seven dead Kalith lying on the ground right behind him. It was understandable why Safara was terrified for her people, but things would never change if someone didn't take the first step. Eli couldn't stand the thought of her living in this fear for the rest of her life, especially when he wouldn't be there to help keep her safe.

"Safara, we need to give the man a chance to explain

himself, but not here."

Her emotions were running hot, but at least she agreed. "I'll listen, but my father should also be part of this discussion."

The Paladin was already nodding. "We'll take care of things here. Unfortunately, we have plenty of experience dealing with incidents like this. Afterward, we'll meet you wherever you think is best."

When Safara didn't immediately offer any suggestions, Eli decided for the both of them. "I'll give you directions to my cabin. It's not far from here. Safara, my two friends, and I will meet you there. Hopefully, Chief Dennell will join us as well."

"Give us a couple of hours. By the way, what do you want us to do with the mystery guy over there?"

"Bring him along. We might as well make a party of it." He glanced back toward the truck. Their captive had managed to sit up and was watching them.

Hunter joined the conversation. "Any idea what his game is?"

Eli nodded. "He might be part of a group that's been dogging my heels for a while now. If so, either he or one of his buddies ran my friend off the road earlier today."

Lonzo rubbed his jaw. "Interesting. Any idea why?"

If Eli expected Safara to give these men a chance, he needed to do the same. "Maybe because I died in a military helicopter crash a few weeks back."

He had to give it to these guys. His little bombshell didn't faze them at all. Instead, Hunter smiled as he stepped closer and held out his hand. "I'm guessing you have some questions of your own. We'll be glad to answer them."

Eli shook his hand and nodded. "Good to know. We'll go pick up our friends and head for the cabin."

Safara nodded toward the tarps. "What will you do with . . . with them?"

She'd addressed her question to Lonzo, but it was one of the Kalith who answered. "We will return them to Kalithia. We have contacts there who do their best to identify the bodies and return them to their families for burial."

Her shoulders slumped in clear relief. "The one on the far end is named Tiel a'Lyr. He has parents and a brother still living in Kalithia."

Larem gave her a solemn nod. "We'll let our friends know."

By now Safara was looking more like her usual self. "One more thing. They attacked some civilians. They're over there out of sight now, but they saw enough. We have to do something about them."

Lonzo shrugged. "We'll do our usual song and dance. We have badges we can flash, and the Regents have processes in place that will back us up. Hunter, can you take lead on that while we get busy here before anyone else shows up?"

The other Paladin stepped forward. "Will do. Eli, you want to show me where they are?"

Before they started walking, Barak spoke for the first time. "You'd better leave your weapons with us. I promise to treat them with care and will return them when we see you later. Civilians get a little twitchy when they see folks carrying around bloody swords."

Safara shuddered and surrendered her blade. "Thank you."

They made their way across the field with Hunter. Along the way, Eli wrapped his arm around Safara's shoulders and was pleased when she reciprocated by slipping hers around his waist. He adjusted his longer stride to match hers as they fell into step together.

Mike and Doc looked pretty damned relieved to see them. Doc was just finishing up bandaging the arm of a young woman when they arrived. Eli and Safara hung back and let Hunter take the lead. He quickly reassured the civilians, telling them that the danger was past and the culprits were being transported for processing. He made it all sound so official that the people didn't have any trouble accepting him as the real deal.

It was time for the four of them to head out. "If you have no further need of us, we'll be going."

Hunter flashed him a quick smile. "See you soon."

At least Mike and Doc held their questions until they were back in the SUV and driving away. Eli filled them in on what had transpired, answering what questions he could, and making a mental list of the ones he couldn't. After they made a quick stop at the grocery store for supplies, it didn't take long to reach the turnoff to his cabin. Doc dropped Eli off at his truck and then led the way up to the cabin.

Once there, they took turns taking a shower and changing into fresh clothing. When he finished his turn, Eli went out to the porch to join Safara, who was about to call her father. He figured if she wanted privacy, she would say so. When she didn't ask him to leave, he sat down in one of the chairs and tugged her down onto his lap.

The minute she started talking, Eli could hear that her

dad had gone ballistic. He wasn't about to let the man yell at his daughter for making the only decision that made sense in the long run. He snatched the phone from her hand and took charge of the situation.

"Jakes, shut the fuck up. And before you ask, no, I won't give the phone back to Safara just so you can yell at her some more."

He let the man rant a little bit before cutting him off again. "No, *you* listen. You weren't there, so don't second-guess the situation. If those guys hadn't shown up today, things would've turned out a lot differently for your daughter, not to mention the other people the rogues were tormenting. And for the record, the Paladins have been aware of your people for a while now. Sooner or later they would've shown up on your doorstep."

After pausing several seconds to let the man absorb that shocker, he continued. "So here's how I see it. You can haul your ass up here to meet with these guys, or you can hide down there in your office. It's your choice, but one way or another, you're going to have to face them eventually."

Then he hung up and turned off the phone in case Jakes called back.

Instead of ripping into him for his high-handed behavior, Safara shoved the phone into her pocket and cuddled in closer. "I understand why he's worried, but you didn't say anything I haven't tried to tell him for years. Maybe he'll listen to you."

He held her close while he still could. The time was coming when he'd have to walk away. She and her people were going to have enough to deal with now that the Paladins were aware of them. He wouldn't bring his troubles raining down on her head. Maybe the guy in the blue pickup had nothing to do with the black-ops crew looking for him, but the chances of that were pretty minimal.

Safara's thoughts seemed to be running along the same lines. "Do you think that other guy means that black-ops bunch knows where you are?"

"No way to know until we talk to him. It might not have been the smartest move telling Lonzo to bring him up here. But since he'd already found Doc and Mike, it was only a matter of time before he followed them right to my door. I'd rather know what's going on for sure than to stick my head in the sand."

She kissed his cheek. "You mean like Dad has been doing all these years? I would've loved to see the look on his face when you told him that the Paladins already knew where we were living."

It was time for some hard truths. "It will take time for him and your people to trust the Paladins. They will still need to hide their origins from the rest of the human population, but at least they won't be constantly looking over their shoulders for fear that there's a bogeyman following them with a sword in his hand."

He took her hand in his and kissed her palm. "I can't stand the thought of you living in fear for the rest of your life when I can't be here to have your back."

Safara stiffened in his arms and then slugged him on the chest. The blow didn't do any damage, but it was clear he'd said something that she didn't like. "What's wrong, sweetheart?"

"Don't sweetheart me, Eli. We both agreed it was dangerous to get caught up in each other's lives, but you never said you planned to disappear completely."

Her hand settled softly against his cheek. "I don't want to lose you, Eli. Not yet and never completely."

"And I don't want to go."

Her words cut deep into his heart. The thought of never again holding her in his arms made him furious. It was bad enough he'd lost his career and most of his friends. She was all that made this new existence bearable. He turned his face to kiss her palm again, wishing like hell he had something more optimistic to say. "The longer I stay, the better the chance the military will figure out where I am, or those special-ops guys will get their hands on me. Either way, I'll disappear from your life. I'd rather leave on my own terms than be dragged away in chains."

When she sighed and settled back against his chest, he wrapped his arms around her and held her close. These last few moments of peace and quiet would have to sustain him in the lonely times to come. He hoped she knew how much she meant to him. Thanks to his profession, he'd never had the time for any long-term relationships. When it came to the few short-term ones he'd had, never once had he been even mildly tempted to use the "L" word to describe his feelings.

It was killing him to know that the only woman who had ever claimed his heart would be far better off without him in her life. Maybe he was being a coward for not telling her how he felt, but there was no use in admitting how much he cared when he couldn't stick around for the long haul.

Maybe Safara was feeling some of the same frustration.

She captured his mouth with hers, taking the kiss from zero to sixty instantly. He gave as good as he got, trying his damnedest to tell her without words how much she meant to him. Damn Mike and Doc for being inside, because he would've already had Safara in his arms heading right for his bed.

But they were there, and unless he was mistaken, he was pretty sure there were multiple vehicles headed their way. All things considered, he shouldn't be sitting on the porch with his hand up Safara's blouse. She was aware of the approaching vehicles, too, because she gave him one last quick kiss and stood. "I'll go set out the food."

He followed her inside and picked up his gun. Mike joined him at the windows with his weapon in hand until they knew for sure the new arrivals were friendly.

Lonzo's van pulled into sight with Jakes's cruiser only a short distance behind them. Bracing himself for what could be one helluva confrontation, Eli stepped back out onto the porch and prepared to greet his guests.

20

Safara wanted to run to her father's side, to somehow ease his way into this new reality of theirs, but Eli had already taken charge of the situation. Right now her nerves were pretty frayed, so she'd let cooler heads take the lead. She slipped back inside the cabin before her dad even had a chance to get out of his car.

Doc was still in the shower, but Mike had been watching the new arrivals from the front window. Now he followed her into the kitchen. "I see the party has started."

"Yeah, it should be interesting, since my father arrived right behind the Paladins. I figured I would stay out of the way so they could get all the chest thumping out of their systems."

He laughed as she started pulling the food out of the fridge and arranging it on the counter so everyone could help themselves. "Anything I can do to help?"

"You can get the silverware out for me." As she pulled the lids off the various containers, she decided to ask some questions of her own. "How are you and Doc doing with what you've learned about all of this? You know, like the fact that I'm an alien."

He dropped a handful of Eli's mismatched forks and knives onto the counter next to the stack of paper plates she'd set out. "It's a lot to get my mind around, but I can't say I'm surprised that we aren't alone in the universe. I'd like to know how two similar worlds ended up sharing a common border, but I doubt I'm smart enough to understand the physics of it all."

"Not many people are."

Mike leaned against the counter and crossed his arms over his chest. "True enough, but I suspect what you really want to know is if we're okay about you being with Eli. The answer's yes. All of these changes have been understandably hard for him. We in the military are used to being part of a team, to belonging. That helicopter crash cut him off from all of that. Connecting with you provided the anchor he needs. Jamison and I knowing the truth also helps. However, we can't always be here for him without risking leading his enemies right to his door."

Doc walked into the kitchen, his hair still damp from his shower. "Did I hear my name being mentioned?"

Mike answered before she could. "I was telling her that we approve of her and Eli."

The other man gave a sorrowful sigh. "I would only point out that I'm a much better catch, but there's no accounting for taste. Besides, Sarge would kick my ass for trying to get between him and his woman."

She laughed, but only because Doc expected it. Still, it wouldn't hurt to share the truth with them. "Eli plans to disappear completely, hoping to keep all of us safe from the men hunting him. He knows I can't abandon my people, not when so much is changing."

Turning her back to them, she added, "Not that he asked me to go with him."

Both men immediately bracketed her, offering their version of rough comfort. Doc patted her on the shoulder. "Eli is a lot of things, Safara, but stupid isn't one of them. He knows you're the best thing that's ever happened to him. You know it, too."

She sniffled a bit. "I do?"

"Yeah, you do."

That flat statement came from Mike. "And if he doesn't figure it out for himself, let us know, and the two of us will teach him the error of his ways."

He flexed the fingers on his left hand. "This arm might be out of commission, but Doc can hold him while I deliver a stern lecture with my right."

She gave each of them a quick hug. "I might just take you up on that offer. Now, we'd better see what's going on outside."

No sooner did she say the words than a parade of oversized men came strolling in. Her father brought up the rear right behind the two Kalith warriors. She looked past him to see where Eli was, but he didn't come inside. She realized the Paladin named Lonzo was missing as well.

What was going on?

When she started toward the door, her father blocked her way. "Eli and Lonzo are busy dragging some guy trussed up in zip ties and duct tape out of the van. Seems Eli has a few questions for him."

She wanted to be in on that discussion. "Everybody, help yourselves to the food and drinks."

If the guy outside was the one who had run Mike off the road, she didn't care what happened to him. But in case he wasn't, he could probably use a drink about now. She grabbed beers for him, Eli, and Lonzo.

Mike came with her, leaving poor Doc to deal with everyone else. She stepped out on the porch just in time to see Eli drop their unexpected guest into one of the chairs and then callously rip the duct tape off the man's face. Not that she blamed him. None of them had any reason to have much sympathy for the guy, especially if it turned out he was part of the crew who'd come close to killing Mike.

She shoved the beer into the man's shackled hands without saying a word. He downed half of its contents before muttering, "Thanks."

He didn't seem at all concerned about being held prisoner by Eli and the Paladins, which made him either incredibly brave or crazy. He studied each of them in turn, his expression turning hard when he spotted Mike. "Are you okay?"

The major glared at him. "Why do you give a rat's ass how I am? You and your friends did this to me."

The man sat up straighter, his anger palpable. "No, sir, it wasn't me. They're not my friends. Not anymore. I didn't sign on to kill one of our own."

"What were your orders?"

He briefly turned his gaze in Eli's direction. "We were told Sergeant Yates here might not be as dead as everyone thought he was. We were to verify that. If we did find him, we were to ascertain how he walked away from a crash that killed everyone on board."

Eli's answering smile had nothing at all to do with good humor. "I didn't walk away. I died just like everyone else."

Their prisoner's response came flying in from left field, leaving them all speechless. He smiled up at Eli and calmly said, "Huh, so I'm not the only one."

LONZO FROWNED AND leaned back against the porch railing. "Well, hell, I never saw that coming. People with that particular ability are pretty damned rare, and it seems we've found two in one day."

Eli used his pocketknife to cut through the zip ties before offering it to their prisoner. "I'd like to see some proof."

The man immediately slashed his palm and held it out so they could all watch the wound disappear.

Okay, then, back to the questions. Eli started with the basics. "What's your name?"

"As of today, Tyson Dahl."

Evidently Eli wasn't the only one whose identity was fluid right now. "What unit are you with?"

Tyson shrugged. "Recon marines. My current assignment is classified."

Mike crowded closer. "Do I have a target on my back?"

Good question. Depending on how Tyson answered it, he might just get to keep on breathing. While he didn't seem all that concerned about being their prisoner, he was clearly pissed off about what had happened to Mike.

"We were only told to keep an eye on people known to

be friendly with Sergeant Yates, but then you started asking questions about us. One of my former associates decided to give you a friendly warning to stay the hell out of our business."

He flexed his hands, a small smile playing at the corners of his mouth. "He's not like us, Sergeant Yates. It will be a while before he can grip a steering wheel again."

Okay, so this guy could live a while longer. "So I'm guessing I'm not the only one who is AWOL right now."

Tyson actually laughed. "Yeah, although I'm not sure you can go missing from an organization that doesn't officially exist."

Mike snorted. "They exist all right. They operate out of a remote corner of Fort Bragg."

Tyson's eyes hardened to the color of cold steel. "Not anymore. They bugged out. And before you ask, I have no idea where they've landed."

Lonzo gave both Eli and Tyson a considering look. "Have either of you given any thought to what comes next?"

Safara clutched Eli's hand, her pretty eyes so damned sad. Yeah, he'd given the matter a lot of thought but hadn't come up with a single idea that wouldn't rip his heart right out of his chest.

He brushed the pad of his thumb across the back of Safara's hand, not sure which of them needed that small connection more. "Why? Do you have any suggestions?"

"I do, but this discussion isn't for everybody, and I need approval from above before I can say more. I'm going to make a quick phone call to put a few things in motion."

Eli hated the delay, but as a soldier, he understood about

chain of command. Meanwhile, he needed to come to an understanding with their prisoner. He reluctantly released his death grip on Safara's hand. "You and Mike go on inside and get something to eat. The rest of us will be along eventually."

She glanced at Tyson and then back at Eli. "Don't be too long."

"We won't."

Lonzo had already disappeared into the trees, obviously trying to put enough distance between them to prevent any chance of his conversation being overheard. That was fine. Eli had a few things to say to Tyson that should be private.

He jerked the man to his feet and gave him a shove to send him stumbling down the porch steps. He made no attempt to fight back, which didn't exactly endear him to Eli. Right now, he could use a convenient target for his temper.

He jerked his head in the opposite direction than Lonzo had gone and waited for Tyson to go ahead of him. They stopped just inside the tree line. "Two questions. Who were you going to shoot earlier? And what's your endgame?"

Tyson sat on a nearby boulder before answering. "I was going to take out the bastard with the sword threatening that couple and their kids. I don't hold with hurting women and children."

The bald statement rang with truth. Like Eli, the marine had probably seen more than his fair share of how the weak and innocent suffered in this world. He waited for Tyson to continue.

"I've put as much thought into my endgame as you did before you walked down off that mountain." His laugh was bitter. "When I was recruited from the marines, I believed in our mission. But somewhere along the way, there was a change in management and the type of missions we were assigned. Like I told Major Voss, I didn't sign on to hunt our own."

Time for another hard question. "When did you die?"

Another laugh, this one a little more lighthearted. "The first time? I was up on a roof hiding from my foster father, who was a mean drunk. When he dragged me back down the ladder with him, I took a header to the ground. They pronounced me dead at the scene, but I revived on the way to the morgue. That scared the hell out of everybody, me included."

Eli clenched his fists. "Tell me they didn't send you back to that same foster home."

"Not after I told them he deliberately threw me to the ground from the roof. He went to jail while me and the other kids got sent to different homes."

Damn, he hurt for the kid Tyson had been, but he knew better than to let it show. Meanwhile, Tyson continued with his story. "The next time, I was out on a long-range sniper patrol and took one in the chest. I still remember the world going black. The next day, I hiked back to camp bloody but no worse for the wear. That's when I was recruited for the spec-ops group."

Lonzo finally joined them in the small clearing. "It would be easier on all of us if there was an owner's manual that explained all the perks that come hardwired in our DNA."

Eli had been aware of the Paladin's approach. "That would be useful. I would've settled for knowing I wasn't crazy."

Lonzo smiled as he sat down on a large log. "Sorry,

but crazy is pretty much part of the package. Our other sterling qualities include hot tempers, faster-than-normal reflexes, and an immune system that's resistant to pretty much everything. Most of us are above average in height and strength. We have an inborn need to defend the barrier between us and Kalithia, which only gets stronger the more you're around it. That driving need to serve and protect is why both of you ended up in elite military units."

Tyson looked confused. "Where the hell is Kalithia? Sounds like someplace in the Middle East, but I've never heard of it."

At least Eli knew that much. "It's actually another world that somehow butts up next to this one. That's where the crazies with the swords came from."

Lonzo took over from there. "Don't worry, Tyson. If you accept the offer I've been authorized to make you, a peek into Kalithia will be included with the guided tour. For now, just know that our ability to heal stems from someone from that world dipping their toes in the human gene pool."

He held up his hand to forestall the barrage of questions he knew was coming. "I'll explain everything, but not right now. I've still got to deal with Chief Dennell, and it's been a bitch of a day for everybody. I do need to tell you a couple of things before we go inside."

He held up one finger. "Regardless of how this plays out, both of you need rock-solid identities to hide from the folks hunting you. Even if you don't accept the offer I'm about to make, we'll help you with that. When my friends get through, your records will stand up to anybody's scrutiny. If you need help relocating, we can do that, too. We take care of our own."

Tyson didn't look convinced, but Eli was willing to give them a chance. "And what's this offer you've mentioned?"

"There are never enough of us to go around. If you want a job doing the kind of stuff you're trained to do, come work with us. You were born Paladins. Here's your chance to find out what that really means. You'd be based here in Seattle for now. Think it over, and let me know."

Then he stood up and walked away. Eli hung back to give both him and Tyson time to process what Lonzo had just thrown at them.

Tyson looked a bit dazed. "Is he on the up-and-up? I mean, all that stuff about another world—that's crazy talk, right?"

Not all that long ago, Eli would've agreed with that assessment, but not now. "It's crazy, all right. But here's the thing: I've actually been to Kalithia."

Not to mention the woman he loved was born there. "Let's go. I don't know about you, but I'm starving."

Tyson remained silent until they were in sight of the cabin. Then he nodded as if he'd just reached a decision. "What have I got to lose? I'll give Lonzo and company a chance. If it doesn't work out, I can always disappear."

Eli couldn't fault the man for hedging his bets. He pretty much felt the same way. When they walked inside, Safara was hovering near the door and walked straight into his arms. "Is everything okay?"

Considering Lonzo had just offered him a way to stay in the area where he could watch over Safara and her people, even if from a distance, things were a whole lot better than just okay. Hell, just a short time ago, he was alone and afraid to trust anyone. Now he was surrounded by all of these people, some from his old life and some from his new one, all of whom knew his secrets and would protect them.

He smiled down at the woman who held his heart in her hands. "Everything might just be fine."

21

I t was clear from the smile on his face that Eli had connected with the Paladins. Good for him. It would certainly be better than having him disappear completely. She was happy for him. Really. Sort of, anyway.

He and Tyson were in the kitchen piling their plates high with food. Somehow Tyson had gone from prisoner to guest, although she doubted he was really trusted. For his part, he tried to act relaxed while at the same time keeping his back to the wall so no one could slip up behind him. She couldn't blame the man for being skittish. Just like Eli and his two friends, Tyson had been dragged into a whole new reality.

Her father looked happier. When she'd come back inside, he'd been talking with Barak. The Kalith warrior had remained beside him when Lonzo cornered Jakes for a short but intense discussion. She didn't know what had been said, but both men had looked satisfied by the interaction.

Right now, Doc and Mike were having a good-natured argument over the chances of one of the local pro sports teams with Hunter and Larem.

It was odd to feel so alone in the crowded cabin. Maybe it was because she was the only woman, or because she was still struggling with the aftermath of the battle at the park. Add that she wasn't sure what came next for her, and it was no surprise she was feeling so unsettled. She did know that with all the excitement of the past few days it would be difficult to settle back into her mundane routine.

Lonzo said something to Eli, who then glanced in her direction before nodding. A few seconds later, the Paladin appeared at her side, two beers in hand. "Safara, can I borrow you a minute? Let's head out to the porch, where it's a little less crowded. "

"Sure."

She accepted the beer he offered her and followed him outside. He motioned toward the chairs. When they were seated, he took a long drink and then set it down beside him. "This has been one helluva day."

"True enough. A few too many surprises. Some good, some not."

Some awful, but she suspected he knew that.

His next words confirmed that. "I'm sorry about your cousin."

"Me, too. He was a good man. Or at least used to be."

Lonzo nodded. "It was easier for us when we thought all Kalith were just a bunch of crazies, but that changed when we met Barak. He nearly got himself killed saving the life of my boss's wife. Barak is now married to a Paladin's sister, and his sister is married to a Paladin. They adopted a pair of Kalith kids who'd been orphaned when their parents came down with the light disease."

Really? How had they not heard about any of that?

"How did my father take that news?"

"Better than expected, which brings me to why I wanted to talk to you." He shifted in his chair to face her more directly. "How attached are you to being a deputy? I'm asking because I've been authorized to offer you a job with our organization."

She had been taking a drink and almost choked. Lonzo pounded her on the back. "Easy there."

When she could breathe, she asked, "What kind of job?"

"As I told you earlier, we've been planning on reaching out to the enclaves of Kalith living on this side of the barrier. We've waited this long because we were pretty sure they would react about like you did earlier, not that we'd blame them."

Considering their mutual history, she wouldn't apologize for not blindly trusting the Paladins. "For what it's worth, I've been trying to get my dad to find some way to learn if the old ways still held true or if the Paladins would accept us."

He drummed his fingers on the arm of his chair. "This would be a pilot program, because the whole situation is problematic for both sides. We're willing to accept those Kalith already here, but we can't let that change in policy open the floodgates from your world into this one."

That made sense, especially from the human perspective. After all, this was their world. If too many Kalith came across the barrier, the existence of another world would get out. God knows what kind of chaos would ensue.

"So you're looking for someone to tell my people to stay where they belong?"

"Hell no. We want someone to act as our liaison with the Kalith who are already here. You'd make first contact and get the message out that we're not on the hunt. If you're interested, I can set up a meeting with my boss to discuss the details."

This was the second time he'd mentioned his boss without using the man's name. That could only mean one thing: Lonzo worked for the scariest Paladin of them all. The man was a legend among her people, and not in a good way. She swallowed her fear long enough to say, "You work for Devlin Bane."

"I do." Lonzo met her gaze head-on. "And yes, Devlin is every bit as terrifying as you've heard he is, but then we all are. Having said that, he's the one pushing to do this. Besides, if you can handle a man like Eli, you can handle Devlin."

"What does Eli have to do with it?"

Lonzo looked amused. "Maybe I misread the situation, but I figure you two are a package deal."

He stood up and stretched. "I'm bushed. I'm going to round up the others and head out. Let me know what you decide. Eli has my number."

She stayed where she was when he disappeared into the cabin. Her head was reeling from everything that had happened. While part of her grieved over those who had died that day, another part of her celebrated the olive branch the Paladins had extended to her people. She never imagined she could play an important role in helping to open communication between the Paladins and the Kalith already living in this world. Hope tasted sweet, especially when it came to the man who had just joined her on the porch.

Eli tugged her to her feet and wrapped her in his arms. It felt like coming home. After a bit, he asked, "Care to share what Lonzo wanted to talk about?"

She reached a hand up to pat him on the cheek. "You're not jealous, are you?"

"Damn straight I am. Do I need to have a talk with him?"

His breath tickled her skin. It was tempting to tease him a bit more, but too much was riding on the decision she needed to make. "He offered me a job working for the Regents. I'd be helping them reach out to other Kaliths living in this region."

"You'd be great at it. You should accept the offer."

She hoped so. "I plan to. I'm not sure how my father will react, but I think we'd be fools to miss this opportunity. It's not like I'd be the only Kalith working for the organization."

Now for the hard questions. "So what about you? I'm guessing they want to recruit you as well. Will that be a problem for you if I'm working there, too? After all, we promised not to get too tangled up in each other's lives."

As he stared down at her, those deep green eyes sparked hot. "Honey, looking back, we blew past that barrier over peach pie that first day at the park."

Eli brushed his lips across hers. "I know I said I needed to disappear, not just for my sake but for yours. Even with the Paladins backing my play, I'll still be at risk of discovery. If that happens, all hell might break loose. But here's the thing—I'm not sure how I would've ever found the strength to walk away from you. From us."

She kissed him back. "That's good. Otherwise, I would have to park myself up here on the mountain full-time to make sure you didn't go all noble on me and sneak off somewhere to hide. Besides, Lonzo figures we're a package deal. I kind of like that idea."

It was time to step off the cliff. "As it turns out, I love you, Eli Yates Jervain."

His arms clamped down tight around her. "I love you, too, Deputy Safara Dennell."

He claimed her mouth with a kiss that took no prisoners. It left them both breathing hard and wishing the cabin weren't full of people. As they waited for their pulses to come back to normal, his mouth quirked up in a small smile. "One thing, though. Give me a heads-up before you tell your father that not only are you going to quit your deputy job to work for the Paladins, but marrying me is part of the deal and nonnegotiable. I'll want to have my sword handy."

She laughed. "Don't worry. I'll protect you. Besides, I think he figured that out for himself. The good news is that he didn't ask to borrow my sword."

Eli gave her another quick hug. "In that case, let's go run everybody off so we can pick up right where that kiss left off."

"Good thinking."

EPILOGUE

For the first time since the helicopter crash, Eli had a future again, one that included friends, family, and a woman who loved him as much as he loved her. It was all good. Lonzo promised to set up a meeting with Devlin Bane, the head Paladin in the Seattle region.

Safara's father had been the first to leave. On the whole, he'd taken all the news better than Eli had expected, at least the part about Safara going to be the liaison between his people and the Paladins. The jury was probably still out on her relationship with him.

Mike and Doc promised to check in on a regular basis to let Eli know they were okay. Tyson planned to hole up somewhere close by until arrangements were made to bring him to Paladin headquarters.

Lonzo hung back with Eli and Safara to finalize a few details. "Unless something unexpected comes up, you should hear from us in the next couple of days. We can't predict what the barrier is going to do, so don't think we're blowing you off if it takes longer than expected."

They shook hands. "Not a problem. We'll be here."

As they walked outside, the Paladin's cell phone rang. He walked to the far end of the porch before answering it. Whatever the person on the other end of the line said had him pounding his fist on the porch railing. "Fuck! What the hell is going on?"

Eli knew not to crowd the man, but whatever had set him off was serious. He had to know if it presented any kind of threat to him or Safara. "Lonzo, what's up?"

"Nothing I can talk about." He started down the steps. "Guys, we're out of here."

Hunter made no move to get into the van. "What's happened now?"

Lonzo grimaced, his big hands clenched into fists. "Another one of us has gone missing."

Barak looked worried. "Someone local?"

"I'll tell you what I know on the way to headquarters."

The brief conversation had ramped up the tension in everyone, but it was Tyson's grim expression that caught Eli's attention.

"Tyson, do you know something?"

Lonzo spun back to stare at the marine, who slowly nodded. "I might."

Most people would've cringed to have that many large, angry men crowding him. Tyson stood his ground. "I was recruited right after I died that last time, and I've suspected for a while now that I wasn't picked just because of my sniper skills. They do a full physical complete with scans and a shitload of blood tests on potential recruits, and not everybody makes the cut. Based on what I've learned here today, I figure someone has caught wind of the Paladins' existence."

His words hung in the air, leaving everyone else speechless as they considered the implications. Finally, Eli broke the silence. "Lonzo, if you're putting a team together to hunt these bastards down, I want in."

Lonzo let out a slow breath before nodding. "What about you, Tyson? Just whose side are you on now?"

The man in question slowly rose to his feet and came to attention. "I'm on ours."

ACKNOWLEDGMENTS

To Michelle Grajkowski—my agent, my friend, and the best companion on this journey that a writer could ever have. Thanks for believing in me and in my Paladins!

To Laura Waters—it's been wonderful working with you to make this story its bright and shiniest best. Thank you for your enthusiasm and editorial expertise!

ABOUT THE AUTHOR

ALEXIS MORGAN has always been an avid reader, and she loves spending her days with hunky heroes and gutsy heroines. The author of the Paladins series and the Talions series for Pocket Books, she has published more than forty books, novellas, and short stories, including contemporary romances, American West historicals, and paranormal romances. She has been nominated for numerous industry awards, including the RITA from the Romance Writers of America, the top award in the romance genre.